RIVERBEND FRIENDS™

Real, Not Perfect
Searching for Normal
The Me You See
Chasing the Spotlight

Chasing the Spotlight

RIVERBEND FRIENDS™

Sarah Anne Sumpolec

CREATED BY

Lissa Halls Johnson

A Focus on the Family Resource
Published by Tyndale House Publishers

Chasing the Spotlight
© 2021 Focus on the Family. All rights reserved.

A Focus on the Family book published by Tyndale House Publishers, Carol Stream, Illinois 60188

Focus on the Family and the accompanying logo and design are federally registered trademarks and *Riverbend Friends* is a trademark of Focus on the Family, 8605 Explorer Drive, Colorado Springs, CO 80920.

TYNDALE and Tyndale's quill logo are registered trademarks of Tyndale House Ministries.

Unless otherwise indicated, all Scripture quotations are from The ESV® Bible (The Holy Bible, English Standard Version®), copyright © 2001 by Crossway, a publishing ministry of Good News Publishers. Used by permission. All rights reserved.

The characters and events in this story are fictional. Any resemblance to actual persons or events is coincidental.

Cover design by Mike Harrigan. Interior design by Eva M. Winters.

Interior illustration of drama masks copyright © streptococcus/Adobe Stock. All rights reserved. Interior illustration of emoji icons copyright © Marc/Adobe Stock. All rights reserved.

For manufacturing information regarding this product, please call 1-855-277-9400.

For information about special discounts for bulk purchases, please contact Tyndale House Publishers at csresponse@tyndale.com, or call 1-855-277-9400.

ISBN 978-1-58997-650-4

Library of Congress Cataloging-in-Publication Data can be found at www.loc.gov.

Printed in the United States of America

27	26	25	24	23	22	21
7	6	5	4	3	2	1

Chapter
1

THE STAGE IS EMPTY. Only the ghost light glows from center stage, throwing light out in a circle on the black floor. Even though I cannot see in the pitch dark beyond, I feel the vastness of the empty auditorium as I step toward the light. I feel the moment when the light finds my face. It is utterly still and silent. I sing a ballad, of course, because every musical and every Disney movie has *that* song. The song where the main character tells everyone what they want the most. Ariel wanted legs, Simba wanted to be king, Evan Hansen wanted to belong.

My ballad is simple. I want THIS. The stage. The spotlight. An audience that leans forward to listen and hear every story my character wants to tell.

I wish I hadn't argued with my mom about piano lessons when I was younger because if I had taken them when she wanted me to, I'd probably be able to write my own ballad by now. Write a musical starring me and telling my story. Some girls see their life as a movie: long, lingering shots of their mundane and magical

2 || RIVERBEND FRIENDS

moments, their moody feelings. Not me. Hands down, my story is a musical. Sometimes funny, sometimes sad, and plenty of random dancing and bursting into song. If I lived in New York City, I'd see a Broadway show every day. But I don't live in the greatest city in the world. I live in Riverbend, Indiana. Seven hundred and fifty-nine miles away from any Broadway show. I mean, yeah, University of Indiana has hosted many touring companies. But it wasn't the same. Anyone who loves musical theater understands that.

I told my parents repeatedly that the only thing I want—birthday, Christmas, both, whatever—was to go see a real Broadway show. In New York. I even found the cheapest flights, where we could stay and everything. They were sympathetic to my plight and offered morsels of hope that "one day" we will get there. It was too expensive right now.

I knew my wish was akin to asking for a pony to put in our backyard. But at least you don't have to keep feeding a trip. It was a one-time thing.

Who was I kidding? If I got to go to a real show, I'd instantly be begging to go to the next one.

During our conversations, I knew money was only part of their concern. My parents didn't travel often and never very far. They visited family or stayed close to home. Adventurous trips were not in their repertoire. I was the adventurous kid of our family, always pushing to explore and experience. I could imagine that traipsing off to New York City sounded scary instead of exciting to them. They were satisfied with their everyday normal while I was itching to explode out of it. I loved my utterly normal family. But I wanted more.

I brought my arms up and out in a dramatic gesture seen at least once in every Broadway show. Dropping my head back, my heart silently belted out the ballad stanza about how people here don't understand me.

Except for one. My brother, Josh.

A pang squeezed in my chest and my head fell forward as images flipped through my mind. Images of his engagement to Jessica, their wedding, and him moving the last of his boxes out of our house into his own grown-up home. Mom said I needed to give him space now, but I didn't understand why. Just because he got married didn't mean he stopped being my brother.

To banish Josh and my urge to text him, I looked up tickets on broadway.com to see how much it would cost to see *Dear Evan Hansen* for tonight's 8:00 p.m. show. A mere $259. *Sigh. Why did Broadway have to be so expensive? And so far away?*

"Whatcha lookin' at, Amelia?" Six-year-old Emma jumped in between me and my phone, yanking me from the stage back to my basement and knocking the phone from my hand and into the pile of cushions and blankets strewn over the floor. Although we weren't related, Emma looked a bit like me. Her hair was redder than my own, but I had way more freckles than she did.

"Nothing," I told her, letting her little sister Ainsley paw through the blankets for the phone. When she dug it out, instead of handing it to me, she tried to unlock it.

Their sister Parker was pouting on the couch. The girls were getting bored. I was getting bored. My parents were meeting with their parents—Jon and Leah Burfield—so, of course, I was expected to babysit. Usually these impromptu counseling sessions lasted about an hour, but we were pushing two and there was no sign of the adults.

Felix, our giant Labradoodle, rolled around in the blankets. I bent over to give him some good tummy scratches. Emma squatted next to him and joined the scratching. Felix was in doggie heaven.

Then we heard—something. Ainsley looked up at the ceiling.

Someone was yelling—muffled and impossible to understand. I watched Parker's face twist like she was trying not to cry.

"Hey! Let's make up a play!" I said. I put the needle on the *Annie* record I'd listened to earlier and turned it up so they wouldn't hear the muffled yelling. Parker balled herself on the giant gray sectional couch with her head down, arms wrapped around her body. She was eight, and there was no way she didn't know what was happening upstairs. Her parents had been coming for counseling for weeks, and she'd mentioned the yelling problem before. The other girls were younger though, so they were easily distracted.

"What's that music?" Emma wrinkled up her nose, staring at the record.

"It's from a Broadway show called *Annie*," I said.

"I don't like it," Ainsley said. "It's too loud." She covered her ears.

I turned it down, then moved the smaller chairs and glass coffee table out of the way. "Look! We can make up a play! And this will be our stage!" I gestured at the area around me. Ainsley and Emma looked unsure.

"A princess play?" Emma asked.

"Sure. A princess play. Whatever." I cringed, still hearing tense voices upstairs. "What will your princess name be?"

"Anna! Elsa!" they both yelled at the same time.

"Let's make up our own princesses. They can have any name you want!" I said.

"I wanna be Anna!" Ainsley said.

"Elsa!" Emma said.

"Fine. I guess we're doing *Frozen*." I looked around for my phone. Ah. That's right. Ainsley had been trying to open it. When she couldn't get it unlocked, she must have dropped it back into the pile somewhere. I tried to convince the girls to make up their own princess names as I dug through the cushions and the blankets they had pulled out earlier to make a fort.

Emma started singing "Let It Go" really loudly but somewhat in tune. Ainsley joined in, twirling in the open area. Felix joined in the fun. He didn't care what game everyone was playing; he was just certain he had to be a part of it. With them singing and dancing, and *Annie* playing discordantly, I gave up looking for my phone and went over to Parker.

"Do you want to be a princess?"

Parker scowled. Her hair was blonde rather than red, and she had a little turned-up nose and big, angry blue eyes.

I wondered what you're supposed to do in this situation. Saying, "Hey, sounds like your parents are screaming at each other," was what came to mind. I kept my mouth shut.

"Can you get rid of one of those songs?" Parker gave me a pointed look.

I shrugged. "I don't have a record of *Frozen*, and I can't find my phone to play it through the speaker."

Parker rolled her eyes and hit some buttons on her own phone. "Let It Go" started playing, and the little girls cheered and joined in. I stopped the *Annie* record. Much better. Really though, they should know *Annie*. Everyone needs to know *Annie*. It was a classic show. But they were both spinning and singing at the top of their lungs to the favored *Frozen* song. Their voices were loud enough to dull whatever might be happening upstairs.

I dropped on the couch next to Parker. "Nice save. You're quick with that thing. My parents wouldn't let me get a phone until I was twelve."

"Maybe because you can't keep track of it."

Truth. "Ouch. But no. My parents are weird like that."

Parker's eyes dropped to her lap again. *Parents. Wrong topic.* "Do they do this all the time?" I asked, pointing at her sisters.

"All. The. Time. I don't even know why they like *Frozen*."

"Exactly. *Tangled* was my favorite," I said.

Parker looked surprised and happy for a split second. "Me too!"

"Then you be Rapunzel! And I'll be Merida! 'Cause this," I said, pointing at my hair. I jumped up and took Parker's hands and spun her around.

"You can't be a princess," Ainsley yelled over the music.

"I'm already a princess! All girls are princesses!" I said. Parker giggled as I twirled her, one of her hands above her head, her purple skirt flying in a puffy circle.

"You can't!" Ainsley said. "You're too fat to be a princess!"

The music kept playing. Parker kept spinning. And I kept quiet.

"Shut up, Ainsley. That's mean," Emma said.

"You're not s'pose to say shut up! I'm telling Mom!"

"I don't care if you tell Mom. You'll get in trouble too."

The little-girl voices began to sound muffled and far away as I faded back to the stage. I'm standing in the circle cast by the ghost light. I back up, one step at a time, letting the light disappear from my face, body, legs, and finally my feet until I am in the shadows once again. The darkness wraps like a blanket around my shoulders; I could almost feel its weight.

From the darkness I tried to call out, "We are all princesses! No matter what size we are!" But I couldn't get the words to come out of my mouth.

"Amelia?"

The voice popped me back to the present—where I did not want to be.

Mom stared at me, one hand on her hip and a tight smile on her face, while the little girls ran to their parents and threw themselves in for hugs—like they hadn't seen them for days. Ainsley's dad picked her up and ruffled her hair, then quickly left with her in his arms. Mom turned to the other mom and made comments about fighting and how it's normal, but the woman looked as if she was about to cry. Parker and Emma and Mom were talking at once, so I stayed quiet and started cleaning up the room while they gathered their things and left.

Emma ran over, hugged me goodbye, and took her mom's hand to leave. Parker waved and followed them out the door, leaving me alone with Mom. I kept tidying.

"Well, that looked lovely, walking the parents down here to find their children fighting and you staring off into space." She folded the fluffy orange blanket that Emma had used as a cape for about three seconds.

I picked up the smaller cushions and arranged them on the couch the way Mom liked them. Everything in our house was arranged just so. Since Mom used the basement room as often as she used the upstairs to host gatherings, it had to be as perfect as the rest of the house.

Ask. Ask.

It wasn't a good time to ask, but when else would I be able to? I moved the coffee table back and set the legs exactly in place where they had left carpet divots.

"Why does this room look like a tornado hit it every time you babysit?"

Ask. Ask.

"Only when it's girls. The boys like the PlayStation and stay in one place," I said.

"Still. You should try to clean up before we come down. It looks so chaotic." She folded another blanket. "I didn't realize how many blankets we have down here."

Ask. "Miss Roxanne has a cancellation for tomorrow at 3:45. Could I take another voice lesson?"

I kept folding and tried to read her expression.

Mom was quiet as she straightened the shelf of DVDs the girls had dismantled.

Quiet was my least favorite response from her. I was pretty sure my mother didn't have a single impulsive bone in her body. Still, I hoped she would say, "Sure!" and move on without long, drawn-out discussions. I would've skipped Mom and asked Dad directly except it was Mom who was going to have to drive me there. And help me pay for it. *I needed Mom on my side, yet how could she be when I was the one kid in our family who baffled her?*

"You've already had, what, three?" She stopped fussing with things and folded her arms across her perfectly flat belly. She had her wavy brunette hair up in a messy bun, and despite her age and choice of wearing a simple pair of black pants, blue blouse, and white sweater, she looked picture perfect. Effortless and easy, the quintessential elder's wife.

I knew what I looked like at that moment. Her exact opposite. A mass of frizzy hair to hers perfectly coiffed. A pair of red track pants to her tailored ones. A rather dirty vintage T-shirt to her filmy blue blouse underneath a fitted button-down sweater. Bare feet to her Rothy's. I sometimes wondered how I was her kid at all. Josh and Maggie, my older siblings, were more like her. Maggie was intense and driven like Mom. Josh looked a lot like her and acted more like Dad. *Me? It was like I was dropped in from another planet.*

Mom never responded when I exposed my heightened emotions—good or bad. I had to be calm. Rational. "Two. I've only had two lessons. Most people go every week. It's hard to get a spot with Miss Roxanne because she's so good, her schedule is always full." I tried to keep my tone light. I longed to say how badly I wanted to have one of those coveted weekly spots, but I resisted. Barely. If Mom got a whiff that I was arguing with her, she would shut down the discussion.

She sighed. "Millie. We've talked about this. I'm really sorry. Voice lessons aren't in the budget."

I resisted for about two seconds before I burst. "You paid for Josh to do travel soccer. And Maggie got piano lessons and a bunch of stuff for cheerleading." I stopped, unable to share that I was worried about my singing. I could work on acting and dancing at home on my own. But vocals? I was at a loss. I didn't know how to improve without help—actual professional help.

"Millie—"

"Those two lessons really helped me! I know if I could—"

"Yes, we encouraged you children to participate in sports because they teach so many great things about teamwork and perseverance."

"So does theater!" My voice cracked. "And Mom, I don't *want* to do sports. I hate sports." *Settle down.*

Mom's lips tightened.

Yelling wasn't going to help her understand. I breathed in slowly. I held it a brief moment, and then I slowly exhaled before speaking again. "I thought it would be okay to try extracurricular activities of my choosing." I congratulated myself on sounding reasonable.

"If you love singing so much, join the choir or worship team at church. They always take new members. You'll learn so much."

Breathe. Breathe. Don't say it.

"It's not the same thing!"

Well. There it was. My traditional fail. If only I could remain calm for an entire conversation.

She started to walk away.

"Mom? Please? Auditions for the school musical are on Wednesday. I'm not ready. I need another lesson." I clenched my fists, so my nails dug into my palms. I hoped the pain would stop me from saying more.

"You'll be fine for a high school audition. Get this room back in shape, please. I'm having a women's brunch in here Wednesday morning."

As soon as I heard her close the basement door at the top of the stairs, I threw myself onto the couch and screamed into one of the striped pillows. I should not have said anything. I should have waited for a better moment.

Once I found my phone, I texted the Fan4 for moral support. Fantastic 4 is what we finally agreed to label the text group for Shay, Tessa, Izzy, and me only a week ago. Izzy, of course, was the one who came up with it. These three girls were my besties now. Maybe a little over-involved and opinionated at times, but in mostly good ways.

I got an assortment of "sorry ☹" and "that stinks." But while, yes, not getting the voice lesson was frustrating, not knowing how to make my mother understand why it was important was worse. No matter what I did, she didn't take my passions seriously.

So I FaceTimed Josh.

"Hey, Millie Vanilli!" He grinned into the camera. "What's up?"

"Mom doesn't get it."

He laughed. "What? Let me guess. Our mother doesn't understand your insatiable love of all things Broadway? Mills, her idea of engaging with popular culture is watching *The Great British Baking Show*."

I frowned, and he laughed again. "I am sorry though."

"I can't just . . . wait, you know? I want to do musical theater for a career. But I'm already behind. There's this girl at school named Presley who performs in professional productions. And she's only a junior! I have a long way to go to catch up."

"Hey, Amelia!" Jessica leaned in so I could see her and waved. At least she called me Amelia. My family and many of the kids at school were still calling me Millie despite my constant requests to call me Amelia. *Amelia* sounded more mature and professional to me. Amelia Bryan. Yeah. I could see that in a *Playbill* bio.

"Hey, Jess." I smiled but wanted her to go away so I could finish talking to Josh. She was sweet, and I knew she loved Josh—both very good reasons to like her. But she still irritated me because I had to share my brother with her. Always.

I preferred Josh over my sister, Maggie, because he treated me like he actually liked me. Maggie, the sister in between Josh and me, acted resentful of my entire existence. Maggie was a sophomore at University of Illinois, which was fine with me. But Josh getting married and moving out for good? That made home feel a whole lot less like home. Josh had always been the one to jump to my defense. Without him, it was me against Mom—especially since Dad didn't have strong opinions about the whole theater thing.

Everything would be different if Josh were home.

Jessica asked me a bunch of small-talk questions about school, and then she finally left.

"Can you talk to Mom?" I asked.

Josh shook his head. "You know I'm your biggest fan. But this is your battle, kiddo, not mine."

"But she listens to you. She acts like I'm gonna grow out of it or something. Like it's a phase."

"Like the monkeys! Or the owls!" Josh laughed.

"Stop. They were cute, and yes, a phase, but this is not."

"How can she be sure that this passion you've got for theater won't vanish and you'll suddenly want to do something else?" He paused. "No offense, kiddo, but you have been known to do that."

For the rest of the night I thought about what Josh said. He was right. I had popped from thing to thing in the past. But I was more mature now. I knew what I wanted. *But how to convince Mom that I was serious about theater, that it wasn't some silly schoolgirl phase?*

If Mom could see me up onstage for our spring musical, *Peter Pan*, maybe she'd see what I knew. Theater is my calling. My present and my future rolled into one. Then she'd understand.

But it would take more than any old part to convince her. I had to play the lead. I had to play Peter Pan.

Chapter
2

"So. I HAVE A CRAZY IDEA," I announced the second the Fan4 sat down to lunch. Well, technically we weren't all sitting because Tessa was still standing nearby talking to her boyfriend, Alex.

Izzy wriggled with excitement, her brown curls bouncing around her face. "I love crazy ideas!"

Shay looked far more skeptical. She unwrapped her standard peanut butter sandwich, an eyebrow raised.

Tessa, in a cute olive-green jumpsuit that I couldn't pull off in a million years, finally sat down after she waved Alex off to sit with his boy group. "What's happening?"

"Amelia has a crazy idea," Izzy said with a mouthful of pizza.

"Of course, she does." Tessa grinned. Tessa was the resident level head in the group. I know I annoyed her sometimes, but I had mostly won her over.

I took in my squad. My crew. I was the type of girl who usually had lots of casual friends. I'd flit from one group to another.

But when these girls came into my life, I started to see that not all friends are created equal. These girls were different and made me feel safe. We'd agreed to be honest and help one another in real ways. But *honest* and *real* also meant that things could be said that were decidedly uncomfortable. I wanted my friends to always agree with me, but that's not what they did. As a result, I had no idea how they would react to what I was about to say.

I waited a moment, partially for dramatic effect.

"I think I should get a pixie cut!" I said, hands splayed out jazz style for emphasis.

Their reaction was worth it. Izzy froze mid-chew, one cheek bulging with pizza. Shay's mouth dropped open, and Tessa looked like I told her we had to hide a dead body.

I laughed. "Isn't that perfect?"

Tessa shook her head. "No. No, it's not. Absolutely not."

Shay looked like she was trying to speak and kept changing her mind about what to say.

Izzy swallowed her pizza and said, "I thought I knew where this was going, and you still managed to shock me."

"Why . . . just why?" Tessa said.

"This is about *Peter Pan*, isn't it?" Shay had that quizzical look on her face that we had grown used to. She was the most serious one of our group. Quieter, but when she said something it was usually insightful.

I grinned. "Of course! If you can audition in a way that shows the casting director exactly how you would be onstage, it helps them picture you perfectly in that role."

They stared at me, wide-eyed.

"I read an article about it in *Playbill*." I set down my pizza, enjoying their utter confusion. "It talked about how casting directors see types. If you can show them in the audition that you are the right type, it can convince them to cast you in the role."

"Mill. This is high school," Shay said. "Not Broadway. I am

begging you to abandon this idea and come back to the world of common sense."

Izzy and Tessa both raised their hands. "Agreed."

"You guys are no fun. It would be a dramatic and memorable gesture of my unfailing commitment to this show." I figured Shay would think it's crazy but had hoped at least Izzy would get it.

"You can't cut off your hair. Your hair is like . . . you." Izzy demonstrated the bigness of my hair by holding her hands out from her ears. "It makes a statement by itself."

"But Peter is a boy. I need to show how I can look like a boy. Besides. Boy cuts are in right now."

Tessa folded her napkin and took a deep breath. "Imagine getting this short boy cut, going through auditions, and not getting Peter. How would you feel about your hair then?"

I shrugged. "But what if I do get Peter? It'll be worth it!"

"You might be aiming too high," Tessa said. "You're a sophomore. The lead is probably going to go to an upperclassman."

"Exactly! That's why I need to make a powerful statement."

"No . . ." Tessa palmed her forehead. "Help? Someone?"

"I think you're crazy," Izzy said.

"Izzy!" Tessa said. "That's not what I meant."

Izzy gestured at me. "Seniority is what matters in high school productions. Not dramatic statements."

"I've thought this through," I said.

Shay raised an eyebrow at me.

"Seriously. There aren't any girl seniors who are strong enough vocally to pull off the lead. There are a couple who are good enough to be in the show, but they'll get the parts with fewer songs. Kevon is the only senior who will get a lead, and he's a guy. That leaves the juniors."

"So, it will probably be a junior," Tessa said.

"I mean, yeah, unless I do something dramatic to tip the odds in my favor."

"Everyone is saying Brie will get Peter," Shay said. Tessa shot her a look, but Shay shrugged. "It's true, isn't it? I've heard a lot of people say that."

I knew my idea was crazy, but part of me thought they'd at least get it. However, the looks on their faces were not ones of understanding. Or support.

"That's why I need to show Ms. Larkin a different look. So she can visualize someone like me as Peter."

Tessa considered this for a moment. "Why don't you audition and see what happens? You can always cut your hair if you get the part. But you can't go back if you don't."

I concentrated on my pizza, feeling hurt. No one said anything more about it until the bell rang.

"We agreed to be honest with each other, right?" Shay said to me as we stood up.

"Yeah. I guess," I said. I turned and left quickly, tossing my trash into the can on my escape to the bathroom. I wanted the girls to be on my side and support me, but I didn't need their approval for a drastic haircut.

The bathroom was busy for a few minutes as people rushed in and out. The second bell rang, and I stayed. I was rarely tardy, but I needed a minute. Because Drama 2 came next, I thought Ms. Larkin would be chill about my late entrance.

When the last person left, I balanced my backpack on a sink while I twisted my frizzy mane and pulled it back and up to get a better idea of how I'd look with short hair. I'd look very different, that was for sure. I frowned. There was another potential problem I hadn't thought of before. It was doubtful my hair would lie Peter Pan flat.

I let go of my hair and hoisted my backpack.

During Drama 2, as Ms. Larkin talked about the audition requirements, I sized up my competition again.

Jenna Ashcroft, Presley Maldonado, and Brie Han sat on the

floor in a triangle—as usual. Though they were juniors, they were positioned solidly in the popular set at Northside High—even among the seniors. They also happened to be widely seen as musical theater royalty. For good reason.

Presley was a pro. Everyone knew that she had performed in shows at our local dinner theater, making her the only person in our school who had been paid to perform. Presley had the tall, lithe build of a ballerina and beautiful dark, wavy hair. She looked like a model in every picture she posted on Instagram. I'd be shocked if she didn't get Tiger Lily. Tiger Lily was the Indian princess who comes to help Peter fight the pirates. It's mostly a dance role, and that was where Presley excelled. She'd be perfect for the part.

Jenna had gotten a really good role in *Seussical* last year as a sophomore. Her legit talent could blow me out of the show, but we looked very different, so that was good. If I were casting, I'd say she looked most like Wendy, the demure older sister. Jenna wasn't demure, but she could play demure for sure. Put a headband on her, and she'd look like a blonder version of the animated character in the Disney adaptation of the story.

Then there was Brie. I didn't notice her much in *Seussical*, because she was part of the ensemble. But this year? Shay had been right. I heard people throwing around Brie's name from the moment *Peter Pan* was announced. I wasn't an idiot. I knew why everyone was saying she'd get the part. With her short, dark bob and petite frame, Brie was the typical look for Peter. I found this kind of reasoning nothing short of infuriating. *Why did everyone assume Peter should be cast based on the fact that a person happened to be petite and know gymnastics? There was more to being a lead than body build or fancy tricks. A whole lot more.* And I didn't know if Brie possessed those qualities. This was our second year in drama together. I hadn't heard her sing, and she wasn't a great actress. She seemed stiff and awkward in class, especially when she was onstage.

I was the opposite of Brie in every way. I was confident onstage, passionate. In Ms. Larkin's classes, she often used me as an example of the expressive energy needed for acting.

So what if I didn't look like the traditional Peter? Sure, everything about me was big. I had big, wild red hair. I had a big body. I liked to say I was "fat and fabulous" in front of people and laugh about it. I talked about how being big was in style to make it seem like I loved the way I looked. I exuded body positivity!

There were days I almost believed my own hype. Honestly. But the moment *Peter Pan* was announced, I started to feel uneasy. *Could being big hurt my chances?* Nowadays, I reminded myself, professional theater was about blind casting and opening up roles to everyone. *Why wouldn't this situation apply? Certainly Ms. Larkin wouldn't cast Brie as Peter just because of her looks, would she?*

I had been hoping and praying that the show was going to be something like *Hello, Dolly!* or *The Music Man.* I could picture myself playing Dolly or Marian. But Peter? I would be foolish not to admit it was a stretch. It gave me a sick feeling to admit that how I looked really could affect—everything.

I walked over to the girls and sat down kitty-corner to their triangle, getting as close as I could. I wanted their reputation to rub off on me. To be seen as a part of their royal court. "You guys nervous about the audition? I'm totally nervous!" I said, ignoring the fact that they had been super mean to Izzy when the Dropbox stuff went down, presuming Izzy had really posed for a topless photo that made the rounds on social media. In reality her boyfriend, Zac, had photoshopped the picture when she'd refused to send him one. Izzy discovered Zac and some of his buddies had created a Dropbox porn site that they sold access to. These girls had never been mean to me directly, so I needed to give them a chance, right?

They looked surprised that I joined them, but I didn't care. I wasn't going to become friends with them unless I tried harder.

"Definitely nervous," Jenna said.

"You? No way! This is your third year auditioning, right?" I scooched in a tiny bit more when Brie moved her bag aside. It was amazing what being forward and friendly could do.

Jenna pulled her legs up to her chest, wrapped her arms around them, and narrowed her eyes at me. "I'm always nervous."

"What are you singing for the audition? I'm doing 'Waving Through a Window,'" I said.

"Me too," Brie said. "I love *Dear Evan Hansen.*"

Mental note: change my song.

"'Dead Mom,'" Presley said.

"'Home,'" Jenna said. "Probably. I mean, I'm still deciding."

She was smart not letting on what her song choice was. No matter. I already knew I needed to change mine.

"Didn't you have some kind of . . . episode at tryouts last year?" Jenna asked.

Presley and Brie snickered.

"Oh yeah." I paused. No one had directly made a comment to me about it before. I shrugged and put on a sad expression. "Crisis at home," I lied.

Their expressions changed like they felt a little bad about snickering, so I laid it on a little thicker. "Yeah. It's better now, but it was a hard time for our family."

"Ohhh," Brie said. "Well, I'm glad things are better." She gave me a genuine smile. In that moment I could picture myself hanging out with them. Being friends with them. That could be amazing. To be in pics with them. Getting noticed and liked everywhere I went. To be considered one of the musical theater girls. So I couldn't let them know how close they were to the truth about what happened.

The real story was that I was standing in the wings waiting for my turn to audition. I had practiced my song for weeks, excited to finally be in high school and participate in the spring musicals.

Then the guy before me, a senior named William, sang "Go

the Distance." It was so ridiculously good that I couldn't make myself take the three steps to the stage, then the few steps more to stand center stage in front of the skinny microphone. I froze. I couldn't follow William's amazing performance because I wouldn't measure up.

My body then decided to freak out. My heart pounded and my chest tightened like someone had wrapped me in a body-sized tourniquet.

I thought I was going to die.

I know how overly dramatic that sounds, but I truly wondered if a fourteen-year-old could have a heart attack.

I had turned toward the darkness offstage and stumbled past Mrs. Copeland, who was helping with the auditions, unable to answer her questions and confusion. I pushed open the stage door. Kids lined the halls waiting their turn, watching me zip on by. I managed to keep moving to the front of the school where I texted Mom and asked her to come get me. It was awful.

Later, I was so mad at myself for freaking out. And I couldn't get away from my stupid failure. From the moment Ms. Larkin posted the cast list, talk about the musical became incessant. Instagram and Snapchat and every kind of social media you could think of filled with pics and comments and inside jokes, reminders that I could have been a part of this amazing event—far more than what little I did as a Drama 1 student. I decided, *Never again.*

I leaned forward and loudly whispered, "Want to know my crazy idea?"

Presley stretched out her long legs and turned like she was finally interested in the conversation. Jenna lifted her chin and looked intrigued. Brie said, "What?" She always seemed to be a step behind the other two.

"I'm thinking about getting a pixie cut!"

They paused and stared at me, like they were trying to decide what it would look like. "You should totally do it." Presley gave me a nod, then nudged Jenna to look at Dev and Hayden goofing around with the juggling balls.

"I don't know . . ." Brie said. "That's major. You can't come back from that if it goes wrong."

"You should do it," Jenna said. "It's so brave of you, and it will be the talk of the school. The bravest thing I've done with my hair is balayage instead of highlights. She smiled, and I couldn't exactly decide if it was genuine, but I had no reason to believe it wasn't.

The bell rang. Jenna gathered her things, tossed her perfectly balayaged hair over her shoulder, and said, "See ya tomorrow."

Chapter
3

THOUGHTS ABOUT CUTTING MY HAIR—do it or don't do it, yes-no, yes-no—consumed my brain the rest of the day. After my final class I found Shay waiting at my locker with an expression on her face that could only be described as horrified.

I was almost afraid to ask. *Was someone dead? Dying?* "What's wrong?"

Shay opened and closed her mouth several times before she whispered, "She said no."

"Who said no?"

"Ms. Larkin."

"To what? What are we talking about?" My utter worry for her morphed into utter confusion.

"She says I have to." Shay's face screwed up like she might cry. Which Shay never did.

"You have to what?"

"Audition." She choked out the word. "For the show."

"But you're going to be working tech and building sets pre-show. You're already involved." I was still confused. We didn't have that requirement last year.

"For class. Remember she said everyone in Drama 1 has to audition? It's two test grades. 'Easy test grades,' she says. 'Show up, audition, and collect two 100s.'"

"She won't let you out of it?"

She shook her head. "She said it would be good for me!" Shay threw her arms out. "I'm going to fail two tests because there is no way I can audition."

All the normal encouraging things that I would automatically throw at Shay were caught up in my throat remembering how hard it was listening to William sing last year. How hard it was to make myself go out on that stage. And I had *wanted* to audition. *How could I help someone overcome her fear when she didn't even want to be in the show—or any show ever—in the first place?*

"We'll figure it out. I'll help. We'll pick a really easy song and practice, and you'll be fine!" I said cheerily, but she shook her head harder. "Look. Let's deal with the getting ready part, and we'll deal with the auditioning part later. One step at a time."

She still looked devastated, but after a really long pause she whispered, "Okay."

"Okay!" I practically yelled. "When can you come over?" The auditions were Wednesday and Thursday with callbacks on Friday. It was important to me that I audition on the first day—it was always best to go early or late—never in the middle. But that only gave us two days, including right then, and I was concerned it might require both days to get anywhere with Shay. She had already overcome a lot just surviving Drama 1. An audition was a whole other level for her.

"Now? I guess? I said I'd help at the bookstore, but Aunt Laura will probably be okay with it. It's for school. For two test grades."

Her face wrinkled with worry, and she kicked her cowboy boot repeatedly into the locker as she texted her aunt.

I swapped out my books in my locker. When the door clanged shut, Shay looked up. "Okay. Let's do this."

———⁓———

After we grabbed some chips and water bottles from the kitchen, I took Shay to the basement with Felix. Mom had dropped us off and left, heading to a meeting with some woman in crisis from our church because that was like a full-time job for her.

Shay had silenced her terror and launched into logical mode, explaining why Ms. Larkin wasn't being reasonable and how Shay had proved herself multiple times this year already and how that should be enough for Ms. Larkin. It made no sense to force people to audition who didn't want to be in the show. "Am I right?" Shay asked, fists planted firmly at her hips.

I shrugged. "It doesn't matter what I think."

Shay dropped onto the couch and buried her face in her hands. "I should take the zeros."

"No! It will be fine! It will be fun!"

She looked up and scowled at me with such intensity that I immediately said, "Okay. Not fun. But survivable. You can survive this. It will not kill you."

Shay grumbled something unintelligible.

"Let's walk through what's gonna happen, okay?"

She was still scowling, but I twirled and used some jazz hands until she smirked a little.

"Okay. So after school Wednesday, we'll go to the drama board and sign in. Then we hang out in the back hallway with everyone who is auditioning. They'll call us in sign-in order. One person auditions onstage while the next person waits backstage, and then

the next person is waiting by the door. So you wait at the door, then backstage, then you go. Make sense?"

"Yeah but . . . like on the big stage? Not the stage in the classroom?"

"Nope," I said. "Big stage."

That was clearly not what Shay wanted to hear. "Why? Why do they need to do it there? Why is that necessary?"

I shrugged. "They've always done it there."

"I hate drama. I thought I hated it before, but seriously, this is sadistic. Why do you drama people put yourselves through this?"

I cringe-smiled. It was a valid question. With no good answer. I waited a beat—like all good actresses, paying attention to the best timing to present the next line. "Once the first fifteen students have gone, that group will go to the band room and learn a dance."

Shay leaped up from the couch. "Dance? DANCE? I thought it was just singing!"

"It's a musical. With singing. And dancing." I did a little ta-da step and jazz hands again.

"Nope. Nope. Absolutely not."

"It's not that bad, I promise. A thirty-second song onstage, maybe twenty minutes in the dance room, and you'll get a 100! Twice! And I'm pretty sure they don't care if you stand in the back of the room and not dance. If you're there, it counts as an audition. And then you're done."

Shay dropped back to the couch.

"Shay, for real. Two test grades? If you don't do this, it'll kill your grade."

She took a deep breath and blew it out really slowly.

"I promise. You will not die."

She twirled her finger in a circle, prompting me to keep going.

"Okay! What songs do you know?"

She shrugged. "I don't even sing in the shower."

"How about 'Happy Birthday'? Everyone knows that one."

"And everyone sounds horrible doing it."

She had a point.

"'Twinkle, Twinkle, Little Star'?" I suggested.

"Seriously?"

"Yeah, people do it all the time."

Shay paused to think about it. "Maybe I could do that one." She didn't sound terribly convinced.

"Yes! Yes, you can! Let's sing it together right now."

We sang it through a couple of times, and I didn't say anything about how her expression looked like she was being actively tortured. That was okay. She didn't want a part anyway.

I pulled her off the couch and had her stand in front of the television. I went back to the couch. "Ms. Larkin, Mrs. Copeland, Mrs. Rinaldi, and Mr. Thompson will be in the audience for sure. Maybe a few senior students, depends on who is helping out."

"That many?"

"You won't be able to see them." I hoped not anyway. I didn't get far enough onstage last year to tell for sure. The auditorium was dark, and the stage was lit, so I thought it was a reasonable guess. "Once you get to the microphone, you slate."

"What?"

"The introduction. You know, 'Hi! My name is Shay, and I'm going to be singing "Twinkle, Twinkle, Little Star" today.'"

"Why does everything involving theater have to have some weird name?"

I shrugged.

"Fine. Hi. I'm Shay. I'm going to sing 'Twinkle, Twinkle, Little Star.'"

She said it so flatly that I almost laughed, but I resisted the urge.

"Then start singing."

After what seemed like ten minutes of her standing there, she finally sang it—practically under her breath, but she did sing it.

I clapped enthusiastically, and she rolled her eyes.

"I know it wasn't good."

"It doesn't matter. That's all you have to do. You're not trying to get a part so who cares?"

"Your turn." She pulled me off the couch and sat in my place. "Let me hear yours."

"Oh, I'm not ready. I still have a lot of work to do. And I'm not sure which one I'm singing. I had one planned but then found out Brie is singing it, so now I'm not sure."

"Why are you being weird? You made me sing. Just sing the original song."

I took a deep breath. I promised myself, over and over, that last year's panic was a one-off. It would not happen again. It was the singing I had been nervous about, and I had worked hard to improve—mostly on my own—so I was more ready this year.

No matter how many plays I had been in, it was the big stage musical I longed for more than anything. Our little One Acts in the fall had only family and friends in the audience. But everyone—the whole town—came to the big musicals. I would not miss my shot this year.

I thought a moment and then pulled up the track to "Matchmaker" from *Fiddler on the Roof*. Whether or not I chose this song, the practice would do me good. I focused on a spot above Shay's head and sang it through. The last line was off. I could hear it, but I wasn't sure how to fix it.

Shay applauded. "You make it look easy."

"It's not," I said. "I'll be super nervous too!" I thought about telling her about my panic last year but decided that would not help. Maybe after we both finished our auditions.

Shay considered me, then asked, "You're not really going to cut your hair, are you?"

"I'm not sure yet. Jenna and them thought it was a great idea."

"Well, I think your hair is fabulous the way it is."

"Thanks."

"You said there's lots of good parts in the show, right?" Shay asked.

"Yeah."

"Getting any part as a sophomore would be good, right?"

I didn't like her logic. "I guess. Ms. Larkin loves me, and she knows I can act. But I still need to help her imagine me as Peter . . ." I trailed off. Shay wouldn't understand the pros and cons discussion regarding "look" in the casting process. Instead I talked Shay into practicing a few more times before she had to go.

At dinner, Mom and Dad talked about the elders' meeting on Tuesday night while I pushed my lasagna around on my plate. I usually loved to talk. It was one of my favorite things to do. But at home nowadays, without Josh, it didn't seem like I had anything to say. The only topic I was interested in talking about was the musical, which was usually met with polite nods. I didn't want polite nods. I wanted enthusiasm! Excitement! Theater wasn't some simple, after-school activity for me. Maybe it started that way. But now? It was everything.

Would cutting my hair help them see my dedication too?

When there was a break in the conversation, I said, "Auditions are Wednesday, so I have to stay after school. Maybe Friday, too, if I get called back."

"That sounds like fun!" Dad said. "What play are they doing?"

"It's not a play, it's a musical—*Peter Pan*. It's going to be so much fun. We're going to bring in a flying company to have Peter and the kids really fly. I mean, we will if we can raise the money for it. It's really expensive, but we'll do fundraisers and all of that."

"You'll keep your grades up though? It won't distract you?" Mom asked.

"Of course not." I was annoyed. *That would be what she asked.*

"Are you nervous?" Dad took a big bite of a breadstick. He was still wearing his button-down work shirt, but the tie was off, and his light reddish hair was slightly disheveled. Good old Dad. I got my coloring from him.

"Yes! So nervous!"

"Really?" Mom asked. "Why?"

I shrugged. "I don't know. It's scary going out there on that big, empty stage in front of people who can arbitrarily decide your fate. I've heard Broadway stars talk about feeling the nerves."

"Every year I was nervous trying out for basketball," Dad said. "Even when I knew I'd make the team, it still felt like I was being scrutinized during tryouts."

"Exactly."

It was the perfect time to bring up the idea of a drastic haircut, but I didn't. I hadn't fully committed myself to it. I was close, though. There was an Instagram account for a Broadway actress I loved, and she was always posting advice from "Aunt Lesli." One time she posted "Go into the audition like the part is already yours."

I planned to audition like the part was already mine. I could see myself as Peter, the boy who doesn't want to grow up. He was sassy and wild and spontaneous. Just like me. Besides, I'd had endless one-sided conversations with God about it from the moment Ms. Larkin announced the show—even before. I felt certain the part was mine. After all, I reasoned, God had clearly led me to drama, which had changed me so much over the past year. Since this was like the next obvious step in my personal and professional growth, I was sure He planned to continue that growth by giving me the part of Peter. Our pastor taught that our outside actions show that we have faith inside. We believe what God has said. For me, cutting my hair could be that show of faith.

Chapter
4

TUESDAY MORNING, I was no closer to making a final decision on my hair, although I had raided and pocketed my babysitting money, taking enough for a basic haircut.

After school I helped Shay practice her song again at my house. And, despite the fact that she was still irate about the required audition, she wasn't arguing about it as much.

We had a snack before I walked her to the bookstore. We said our goodbyes, and then I went a few doors down to the Bella Salon. I stood at the window for a while, watching as stylists deftly held up wet strands and snipped them. Painted foiled hair with goo. Waved blow-dryers to create the perfect style for the customer. Watching women leave looking fresh and beautiful.

I took a step toward the salon door. Then stopped.

Should I?

A haircut like this—no matter what the circumstance—was a huge step. Like Izzy said, my hair was "my thing." A part of me. A part of my personality.

What would I look like? What would my hair do without the weight holding it down?

If I stood just so, I could see my reflection coupled with a stylist cutting a little boy's hair. Everything about me looked big. Felt big. My hair. My clothes. My body. My voice. My laugh. *Would having short hair make me look better? Or worse?*

There was really no way to know for sure until it was done.

I took a deep breath and pulled open the door.

"Hi there. Do you have an appointment?" An older woman with a rounder body like mine greeted me from behind the tall desk. She could barely see over it.

"No. I uh . . ."

"It's okay! Walk-ins are fine. Is there someone in particular . . . ?"

"No."

"All right." She looked around the salon. "How about if I have Ava help you?"

A tall woman with shoulder-length smooth black hair, the ends dipped in purple, walked over. She beckoned me to follow her. "Hi! Come on back!"

I walked behind her, panicking. *Should I do this? Was it too late to change my mind? Would my mother kill me?*

I sat in the chair, and Ava spun me around to face the mirror. A blue drape billowed over me, and she fastened it tight around my neck. She ran her fingers through my frizz. "You have a lot of hair," she said. "What were you looking to do today?"

"Umm. A pixie cut?" I said.

Ava made a duck face as she looked in the mirror. She appeared to be trying to imagine what it would look like. "You sure?"

"Why?" I managed to ask.

"You have a—a lot of volume. If I cut it to here," she said, demonstrating with her fingers, "it will likely be"—she held both hands out—"like a bush."

"Oh." As determined as I was, that sounded awful.

"It's your hair though! If that's what you really want, I will make it work!"

"Really? You can do that? Even with my hair?"

She nodded. It was a slow nod, not an enthusiastic one. Ava twisted my hair and then puffed it so it would fall around my face.

"Maybe not full pixie? We do maybe . . . here?" She let my hair fall around my ears.

"Okay," I squeaked out the word.

What else could I do? I was already sitting in the chair.

Yes.

I could do this.

It would show everyone—Ms. Larkin, my parents, my friends— how serious I am about becoming Peter.

"You have enough length to donate your hair. Would you like to do that?"

I could only nod. A band of fear tightened around my chest, and I couldn't quite take a deep breath. I was adventurous in many ways, but I had never done anything so drastic with my hair before. I watched her in the mirror with curiosity as she put my hair into four pigtails. Then a mixture of horror and disbelief flooded me as she snipped them off. It was like I was watching it happen to someone else. I wanted to scream for her to stop, but I had become a rock, solid and unmoving.

When she took out the little rubber bands, it got worse. Much worse. I looked like someone who had been lost in the woods for weeks and emerged frazzled and confused.

Ava smiled at my stunned expression. "Oh, we'll clean this up!"

I let her walk me to the shampoo area and wash my hair while she chattered about who knows what because I wasn't listening. I was imagining multiple scenarios about what my parents were going to say. All of them ended badly.

Yep, Mom was going to kill me.

It was too late to turn back. It was done. My hair. This red frizzy part of me was lying on the counter. It felt like she had chopped off an actual appendage.

Did my hair really make me me? *Like Izzy said? Then who am I now?*

Oh my gosh, what would people say at school?

Would I look desperate? A desperate wannabe?

I had meant for the bold haircut to make me appear strong and confident. *But what if I now looked the exact opposite?*

My throat tightened, and my eyes burned. I refused to cry. The haircut was a good thing, I told myself. A huge thing. But a good thing! A brand-new me! It was going to be great!

I survived the rest of the snipping and clipping by clenching my teeth together and forcing myself to figure out what song to sing for my audition. I couldn't sing the same one as Brie, and I didn't like how off-key that last line came out in "Matchmaker" from *Fiddler on the Roof*.

By the time Ava started to blow-dry it, I had decided two things. One, I would sing "I Cain't Say No" from *Oklahoma!*

And two, I made a huge mistake.

———

Ava talked me through how to use a fat round hairbrush to blow-dry my frizz into a smooth, styled version. My eyes burned again. My hair didn't do what my imagination had designed. The picture of the cute pixie cut was not what I saw in the mirror. Not only could I not describe the cut, but I also didn't know who I was looking at!

I managed to give Ava a tight smile and a nod when she asked me if I liked it. I paid and got out of the shop before I fell apart.

Outside, away from the mirror, I could almost pretend I hadn't done it. But my scalp felt relieved of the burden of heavy hair, and a small breeze breathed on the back of my neck.

I thought about going to Booked Up to get moral support from Shay, but she would definitely put me in the category of insane human being. I couldn't cope with her questions about why I did such an impulsive, irrational thing.

She would be right.

I texted Mom to pick me up, and I paced around the outdoor mall looking in the windows, trying to convince myself the cut would be awesome. It was awesome. Not what I imagined exactly, but still a dramatic gesture.

When Mom pulled up to the barricade at the end of one of the closed-off streets, she stared, mouth agape, blinking fast like maybe she was seeing things.

I dropped into the passenger seat and looked straight ahead.

"What . . . what have you done?"

"I don't want to talk about it," I said. I didn't look at her, but I could imagine her expression quite clearly.

I could feel her unwavering gaze. "Oh, you'll talk," she said, fingers tapping the steering wheel. "I need an explanation. Now."

I shrugged. "I just wanted to." I knew I would never be able to articulate my reasons to her.

"You just wanted to? Since when are you allowed to do something like that without asking?"

"You would have said no. You never let me do anything I want." It was a dig, but I couldn't help myself.

"And that was disrespectful."

"Sorry," I muttered. She pulled away, and I stole a glance at her. She was shaking her head in disbelief, her lips pressed together.

Why was she mad? It was my hair, and I paid for it myself. I was the one who was going to have to live with it.

But I didn't say any of that out loud. I was already in danger-ous territory.

"I didn't know I had to ask to cut my hair," is what I did say because it was true. But I could hear the bite in my words.

"Just because we never specifically said 'you have to ask permission to cut your hair' is no reason to assume that you don't need to ask. I've never told you that you had to ask permission to do lots of things, but I assumed you would use common sense. I guess not. Did you pray about this? Why don't you think before you do things?"

"I did think. And I did pray."

"Not enough. You look . . ." She trailed off. I wasn't sure if she stopped because she wasn't sure what to say or because she knew what she wanted to say but decided not to.

"It's just hair," I said. More to myself than to her.

It will grow back, I told myself. *It* will *grow back.*

"I don't know what to do with you," she said.

I sat there, not wanting to make the situation worse than it already was.

Mom pulled in our driveway, put the car in park, and turned toward me. "Why?" she asked again.

I sighed. "You wouldn't understand."

"Try me. I can't get my mind around the fact that you did something like this."

"It's not permanent. It'll grow back."

"In a year or two maybe."

"I donated it. It helps kids with cancer."

"Is that why you did it?"

"No."

"Amelia. Come on."

"You're not going to understand, so what's the point of talking? It's done. You're mad. I can't fix it."

"I'm not mad," she said.

Yeah, right. She was mad. And I broke another unknown rule.

"I'm really trying to understand, but you've got to help me. Does this have something to do with your play thing you want to be in?" she said.

"It's a musical, not a play," I yelled. *If she couldn't get that straight, how could she understand anything else?* I couldn't stop myself. "I've tried to talk to you. Over and over. If you don't understand why it's important that I take voice and dance lessons, you're not going to understand this." I got out of the car and went to the house. It was a risky move to walk away, but I couldn't deal with it anymore. Especially since this time I was pretty sure I was as horrified with myself as she was with me.

—⁓—

Dad was at the kitchen counter looking at his computer. I moved quickly toward the stairs and yelled "Hey, Dad!" before he could see me.

"Hey, Millie! How was your day?"

"Good. Yours?"

"Fine. See you at dinner."

"'Kay." I walked swiftly to my bedroom, closed the door, and leaned against it. My safe zone. My bedroom was like me, messy and eclectic. I had the same furniture from when I was a kid, simple and white, but I had changed my room's color scheme from a bright yellow to a rainbow of colors as I added things that made me happy. A pale blue comforter that was like sleeping under a cloud. Throw pillows of every color that drove Mom crazy because nothing was coordinated. My favorite spot in the room was the wall that held nine carefully arranged *Playbill* covers that I had painstakingly collected over the summer at yard sales. Not many people in Indiana had *Playbills* so finding nine was nothing short of miraculous. I was eager to add a real one, from a show I actually saw, to my collection.

It was that spot in my room I looked at first when I came in. A reminder of the goal. But today, instead of making me feel better, they only reminded me about my hair and my mom.

Did you pray about this?

Her question bothered me. I had prayed—a lot—but she assumed I hadn't. On top of that, I had this sneaking suspicion that my family thought that because I was so loud and so different from them, that maybe it was because I didn't pray enough. Like I would *be* different if I prayed more. Or that maybe the way I believed in God was faulty instead of believing in God the way they do.

But even those miscommunications paled when put next to what I really needed them to understand—that there was really one thing that mattered to me. *Peter Pan.* Being Peter would make it clear to my parents how important musical theater was for me. They would see, really see, how I came alive onstage. Being Peter would prove that not only was my heart there, but I also belonged there.

I felt like God understood that.

Chapter
5

CUTTING MY HAIR was a huge mistake. That much was obvious.

It looked nothing like the boy cut I imagined. I pictured Scarlett Johansson and ended up with Raggedy Ann. I was terrified to wash it because Ava had applied product, heat, and a stiff brush to smooth it. The second water touched it, I knew it would spring back into chaos. As long as the product was doing its work, my hair was lying flat, cut to my chin. The bangs were severe, but they lay flat as well. I would wait as long as humanly possible before I washed it.

I looked so different that I felt like it wasn't me in the mirror. If I lived in New York City, I could probably pull off this strange look. In fact, it could be kind of chic. Combined with my typical outfits, I could walk down the city streets with nary a glance my way. *But in Indiana? At my high school?*

I pulled out my vintage oversize Ramones T-shirt and my favorite plaid pants—since it was finally warm enough to wear them. Relatively anyway. My lucky pants. Mom got mad at me when I used the word *luck* because she'd launch into a spiel about how there was no such thing as luck. She didn't get that it was just a saying. And I wasn't talking about *luck*. When I wore these pants, I felt better somehow. More me. More confident.

I added a rainbow cardigan to complete my look and glanced in the mirror, wishing the haircut was a bad dream.

—m—

I took the side entrance to the school by the bus ports because I thought there might be fewer students there. Still, I spotted some double takes, heard some whispers and snickers. I kept my face forward and ignored them. At least this time I didn't hear anyone loudly asking, "Was that an earthquake?" when I went by. Apparently that joke never got old. From about fifth grade onward, it never died.

I turned down the hallway to go to my locker. A jittery Shay hovered nearby. I'd been so sidetracked with my hair crisis that I hadn't responded to her frantic texts. I felt bad that I hadn't, but I didn't have the energy to carry someone else's big emotions as well as my own. Adding to the hair crisis, I was nervous about the audition, but I knew she was far more nervous than me.

The moment she saw me she went from circling to a dead stop, eyes widening, and her jaw dropping open.

I covered the last steps between us and said, "Ta-da!" With a smile. And jazz hands. "Fake it till you make it" was a mantra I would make work for me even if it killed me. I would not admit that I had cried myself to sleep. I would not look to anyone else for reassurance or approval. I'd own it. Every bit of it. I made the choice to get it cut. Now I had to embrace it. There was no other alternative, anyway. Like it or not, this was the new me.

Shay shook her head slowly like she couldn't believe what she was seeing. I understood. Before Shay could find words, I heard someone behind me.

"Noooooooo!" *Tessa.*

I turned to smile at her, too. But my bravado waned a bit because their shocked looks could also be described as a little horrified.

"Yes! What? You didn't think I'd do it?"

Shay finally spoke. "No." She studied me. "When? I just saw you last night."

"Right after I left you. Bella Salon—by the bookstore."

I opened my locker and focused on getting my books for the first few periods to give myself a break from their expressions. *It would be fine. New me. New me.*

"What'd I miss?" Izzy asked. I turned around. Might as well shock all three at once.

"No. Way. No way!" Izzy reached out and touched it. "How'd you get it so smooth?"

"The salon did that. I'm sure it won't look like this after I wash it," I said.

Izzy laughed, "Sorry! I can't help it. It's just . . . you're so . . . nuts. I love it."

"Really?" I asked.

"Sure. Of course, it's going to take some getting used to. Right, girls?" Izzy said.

Tessa nodded slowly, "Yes. Yes, it will."

Izzy gasped. "Oh my stars! I know! You look like a red-haired Edna Mode!"

"Edna who?" Shay asked.

Izzy had already pulled up a picture of the super-suit designer from *The Incredibles* franchise. She held it out for Shay.

Shay checked out the picture and then looked at me. "Yeah. Kinda." She shrugged. "If you decide you don't like it, it's hair. It'll grow back."

"Exactly!" Izzy said. She hugged me. "Oh! And here! These

are for you and Shay! Good-luck cupcakes!" She handed us each a small box.

"Maybe I should wait and audition with you and Tessa tomorrow," Shay said. "I'm not sure I can—"

"Let's get it over with!" I said. "The more time you think about it, the worse it'll get." I put my hand on her arm. "Please don't make me go alone."

Izzy couldn't contain her delight. "You'll be fine, Shay. I'm kind of psyched about *Peter Pan*. It's going to be so much fun! I'm so happy we're doing this together!"

"I'm not!" Shay said.

"Not happy, or not doing it?" Izzy asked.

"Both."

"I'm not thrilled about it either," Tessa said to Shay. "But you'll be backstage helping, so we'll still be together."

Shay looked unconvinced.

"You're totally ready, Shay, and I'll be with you the whole time."

She stared at me for a long moment. "How can I take you seriously with that hair?"

Everyone laughed. Including me.

—⟋⟍—

I started out the day being physically in my classes but mentally hiding in a bathroom. Kids pointed and laughed so much that I felt ridiculous. But I was so determined to be okay with my choice that I took a selfie and captioned it #newme and posted it to Insta. I used the selfie for my Snapchat streaks as well.

In Drama 2, Jenna said it looked cute but only after she snort-laughed about it. Brie and Presley mostly whispered and kept staring at me. I didn't want to know what they were saying. *Or thinking.*

The rest of the day, as much as I could, I kept my eyes averted from everyone. But I stood tall and confident. My hair made a statement. That's what mattered.

I just hoped it was the right statement.

When the 8th period bell rang, I felt pre-audition nerves, but also exhilaration. It was finally happening.

Shay waited at the drama board like we agreed on. We signed our names, hers first and then mine, slots eleven and twelve. My goal was to help her get through her audition—and I totally believed she could—before I did my own. If Shay could get through an audition, then I could too.

Jenna and her crew were going to try to be last on Thursday. Which is what I would have done if I had the nerve. But I knew I'd get in my head too much if I waited, hence my choice to go early on Wednesday.

Everyone signing the board was nervous, and that made feeling my own nerves a little easier. Shay sat with her back against the wall and stared straight ahead, arms wrapped around her knees, tapping her cowboy boots on the vinyl floor. Everything I asked her elicited one-word robo-responses, so I stopped trying to make small talk and people-watched as the hallway filled.

Why did I feel so anxious? I couldn't seem to convince my brain to settle down. I already had the part. Peter was mine. All I had to do was go in there and show them.

A couple of students showed up wearing costumes, which was a big audition no-no. Ms. Larkin had reviewed audition etiquette in her drama classes; no wearing costumes, no singing songs from the show, knowing how to slate. But the musicals were popular, and you didn't have to take Drama to try out, so lots of people didn't know the rules.

Ms. Larkin, always efficient, came out a few minutes before three thirty and explained the process. At exactly three thirty Anthony, the lanky, mohawk-haired senior who helped on the tech team, started calling names, and the first three students took their stations.

When they called Shay's name, what felt like only a few seconds later, her eyes went super wide, but she stood up and walked to the door. I got up and stood with her. "Moral support!" I said to Anthony. "Can I stay with her?"

He shrugged and said, "I don't care."

I linked arms with Shay, as much for myself as for her.

Focus on Shay. Focus on Shay. Don't think about the audition. Think about hers.

Knowing I panicked last year ramped up my nerves.

Mrs. Copeland opened the stage door and beckoned to Shay. I stayed linked and went in with her. Mrs. Copeland didn't say a word. The deeper we moved through the darkness of backstage, the more I was dragging Shay.

"Just like we practiced. Keep it simple," I whispered. "You can do this."

We waited at the edge of the stage until Soon Li finished up. She had a really pretty voice, but she was a freshman, so I doubted she would get much of a part.

We heard the thank-yous, and Shay gripped my arm as if she had turned to stone.

"You're good. You've got this," I whispered.

Shay took a step backward and then tried another, but she'd have to take me with her.

"Come on." When she didn't start moving on her own, I pulled with my linked arm. While she made it very difficult, I kept us both moving toward the pool of light and the microphone stand center stage.

I gently pushed her the final step toward the microphone. She looked terrified, but after an agonizing moment she spoke. "I'm Shay."

Then she sang "Twinkle, Twinkle, Little Star"—with her eyes closed—and then bolted offstage into the darkness.

Leaving me.

Standing there.

Alone.

I was already there. Already on the stage. I only had to take three more steps and speak. This was my shot! I could do this! Shoulders back. Chin up. Smile. I am Peter.

"Hi. I'm Amelia Bryan, and I'll be singing . . ." *What was I singing?* I had changed it. *What had I changed it to?* My heart kicked up a beat . . . and then I remembered. "'I Cain't Say No' from *Oklahoma!*"

"Are you singing a cappella?" The voice came from the auditorium, but I couldn't tell who it belonged to.

"No, I have a track."

I reached for my phone, but it wasn't in my back pants pocket. I patted both cardigan pockets. Empty. *Where was it?* I had no idea.

Well. Great. I did not *have a track.*

"A cappella," I squeaked out.

No worries. I will be professional about this. I don't need music.

I straightened, took a deep breath from my diaphragm, and within moments, I was done.

I smiled again. "Thank you."

I rushed off the stage feeling both excited and a little upset. *I did it!* The first part was maybe a little shaky, but the rest was good. I didn't get the last note right, but it was just one note. If I'd had the music track, I would have sung the song better and not missed that last note. *But that would be okay, right?* Surely they weren't expecting perfection. I only needed to be good enough to get a callback. From there it would be no problem. I knew how well I would do with cold reading the scenes.

Shay was waiting in the dark and grabbed me. We walked into the hallway where the noise and commotion and brightness was a stark contrast to the dark and quiet of the stage. Maddy and Chloe, the choreographer's student helpers, were already lining us up to go learn the dance.

"You're sure I can stand in the back, right?" Shay still looked scared, but the color was returning to her face. I nodded. She took a deep breath and muttered, "Almost finished. I'm almost finished."

I nodded again. But what was going through my mind was that Shay hadn't said anything about my audition. Nothing. I had expected, at the very least, a "Good job!" or "That sounded great." I tried to tell myself that she was too distracted about going into the dance room, but I needed to hear from someone that my song was good. Someone I trusted. Normally I would ask. Instead I fell silently in line behind Shay, and we followed the rest of the nervous kids into the band room where everyone spread out to give themselves enough space to learn the dance.

Priya Madalay scanned the room and smiled as Ms. Larkin raved about how excited she was to have her choreograph the show. Priya was dressed for a workout, her hair in a long dark ponytail. "Please, relax and have fun," she said after the introduction. "I'm looking to see how you move, so just do your best. It doesn't have to be perfect."

I smiled at Shay to encourage her, but she had her arms folded and was practically leaning against the back wall.

Despite the fact that I'd never had any dance classes and was bigger than everyone else in the room, I could follow the steps relatively well. I danced my way toward the front of the room hoping Priya would notice me and see I could do the dancing the musical required.

The moment Priya dismissed our group, Shay bolted from the room, and I followed.

In the hallway, she paced rapidly in little circles, her arms around her waist. "It's over, right?"

I nodded. "Yep. You're all done."

She stopped, dropped her head backward, looked at the ceiling, and raised her hands as though speaking to God. "The depth of my gratitude is beyond measure." She whipped around to look at me. "And I will never take drama again for the rest of my life."

I lifted both hands and shrugged. "I understand. I mean, I don't, but I do."

And then we grabbed our backpacks. I wanted to ask, *"How did I do on my song?"* But I let her go.

Chapter
6

OUTSIDE IT WAS WARM AND SUNNY, and the bus loop where my mother picked me up was empty. I finally found my phone in the bottom of my backpack. *Why hadn't I made sure I had it in my pocket before going onstage? How professional was that?* I took a deep breath, analyzing every moment of the audition as I texted Mom. Replayed it. What I discovered is that I needed a do-over. Desperately.

Mom pulled up and swapped sides so that I could drive home. I slid in and buckled up.

"How did it go?" she asked. Her chirpy voice grated.

"Fine." I adjusted the mirrors and pulled out, thankful the drive home was short.

"That's it? Fine?"

I bit my tongue and gave her a quick nod as my response. It wouldn't do me any good to tell her more than that.

Once in my room, I dropped to the floor and got out my phone. I had texts from the Fan4 in our chat.

Izzy: **How did it go??**
Tessa: We prayed!!
Shay: **I can't believe I'm still alive.**
Izzy: 😂😂😂😂😂😂😂😂😂😂😂

I put down my phone, my stupid phone that I could never keep track of, and considered my audition.

It was good, but having the music would have made a big difference in my performance, I was sure of it. I could have done better, *would* have done better, with the music. It would have helped me settle down and match pitch better. Unless you're on the caliber of Idina Menzel, singing a cappella is not a great choice.

But no matter how many times I reviewed each moment in my mind, I always arrived at the same conclusion. I was worried. "Good" wasn't good enough. I needed "great" to have any shot at the lead.

I kicked off my shoes. And then it came to me. I knew exactly what I had to do.

—⁓—

I got to school early the next day and headed directly to the drama room, trying to maintain my confidence. I had a reasonable case. I couldn't give up without a fight. I had to prove what I was made of.

I took a deep breath and opened the door.

I loved the drama room. Every time I walked in, a sense of *home* washed over me. During freshman year I'd finally found a place in the universe where I could actually be myself. I fit in this world of theater. It was as though I had been born for it.

Ms. Larkin had decorated the drama room to make even the

most timid actors more comfortable. Mismatched area rugs met at odd angles, hiding the standard ugly vinyl tile flooring. Instead of rows of desks or tables facing an intimidating stage, cushy love seats, chairs, and beanbags—and a pink stiletto shoe chair—were strewn about in no particular order. Everything could be rearranged into any configuration at any time. You never knew what the room was going to look like when you walked in. As a result, the stage itself, where we performed monologues and smaller productions, looked more like an afterthought than a focal point. I felt more at home here than in my own house. Walking in this morning gave me the boost of confidence I needed.

Ms. Larkin was at her computer but looked up and smiled when she saw me. I adored her. She was great at making you a better actor and managing to encourage you while doing it. I eagerly embraced and applied everything she recommended. As a result, I felt like we had made a good connection over the past year and a half. I knew she would understand my plight.

"Amelia! What are you doing here so early?"

"I needed to talk to you, before, well, before the day started."

"Okay. Sit. You look a little frazzled. You okay?" She gestured toward a nearby chair and turned in hers to face me. She adjusted her long skirt so it wouldn't get caught in the wheels of her office chair, then folded her hands in her lap. "You have my full attention. What's wrong?"

"My audition yesterday. I . . . I was really nervous, and I know I could have done so much better. Like way, way better. I needed my vocal track to do my best—my phone had slipped to the bottom of my backpack. I would like the chance to show you what I can really do."

That sounded reasonable. Calm. I clenched my hands and watched her face closely, trying to read her expression. It felt like a really long time before she said, "Amelia." And when she said my name, it was in that breathy way that meant she was going to try and make me feel better. My confidence started to drain away, drip by drip.

"Nerves can get the best of everyone! I've heard interviews where famous Broadway stars talk about their pre-audition nerves. You're only a sophomore, and every audition you do will help you grow and get better. That's why you're here!" She reached over and clasped my hand for a brief moment. "Everyone who wants to be part of the show will be part of the show. You have nothing to worry about. You did just fine. You'll find you get stronger each year."

"But I would like to show you how the vocal track would have made a difference. Could I send you a video? Anything? I would love to be considered . . . you know, for a lead." I watched her expression for changes, but she simply patted my hand again.

"Everyone will be considered, I promise. There's a lot that goes into casting."

"I know, but I'd like to show you my best. That was not my best. Please let me prove to you that I can do it."

"Amelia. Trust the process, okay?"

The bell rang behind me, and I knew I had to get to Geometry, but I didn't want to leave. "Please? I'm begging you."

She looked into my eyes without wavering. "I'm sorry."

I got up and bolted from the room, refusing to cry in front of her. I had been sure she'd say yes. *Why was she being so unreasonable? What harm would there be if I auditioned again?*

—m—

In Drama 1, I took advantage of my student assistant status and walked straight to Ms. Larkin's desk without speaking to anyone. I dropped my pack on the floor and sat in the desk chair. I waved to my friends and then indicated the pile of scripts tossed haphazardly across the desk and shrugged as though I had a job to do and couldn't join them in our usual seats today. As I sorted through the scripts, Ms. Larkin explained production design to the class.

I tuned her out, having heard the talk last year. Honestly, I didn't understand what was going on here. I had spent my freshman year taking the Drama 1 class with as much gusto as anyone—if not more. All my hard work had helped me gain more confidence and skill as the year went on.

Ms. Larkin had appeared thrilled that the office assigned me to be her Drama 1 teaching assistant. I eagerly helped her in any way she needed, whether that was making copies or running an errand or helping with the groups. She knew the extent of my commitment. As a result, I thought she and I were on the same wavelength. *So why wouldn't she bend the rules for me?* I needed a second chance.

After class, Shay smiled as she approached. "Hey, glad to see you're alive." She waved her phone at me. "You haven't responded since yesterday. Once I chilled out last night, I realized I didn't properly thank you." She gave a quick bow from the waist. "Thank you for dragging me out there. It was truly horrible, but I'm very glad I didn't tank my grade. That's what I texted you anyway."

"Oh yeah, I don't know where my phone is," I lied. It was so typical for me to misplace the thing that no one would question it.

Tessa and Izzy came over together, and we walked to lunch. Izzy had on blue leggings spattered with shooting stars. Tessa was wearing a flowered shift dress with plain black leggings and boots.

"Maybe we should glue your phone to your hand. Would that help?" Tessa said.

"You probably have a hundred texts from our group," Izzy said as she practically bounced down the hall. "I'm so nervous but so excited. How did it go for you?"

"Oh. I figured Shay would have already told you how awful it was."

Shay frowned. "I was barely paying attention. I was still

recovering from the horror of standing up there with everyone staring at me."

"I'm sure it wasn't awful," Tessa said to me. "I'm sure you did great. We're always our own worst critics."

I frowned, still angry with myself. "I didn't have my vocal track. I could have done so much better if I had." I wanted to tell them about asking Ms. Larkin for another chance to audition, but I couldn't say anything else without potentially dissolving into tears. I didn't want them trying to reassure me that everything would be okay because it wasn't going to be okay unless I got another chance.

"No matter what happens, this is going to be so much fun," Izzy gushed.

I clenched my teeth. Clearly she didn't understand how important this was for me. I could hear her voice along with the chorus of others, including my parents, teachers, anyone really. "Silly Amelia with her Broadway thing." "You're only a sophomore!" "There's plenty of time!"

No one had any idea how much I needed this shot. This wasn't *just* a musical. This wasn't *just* a part. This was my *heart*. My *life*. My *future*.

If I only had some tiny little part, how was I going to prove to my parents that my passion for acting in musicals wasn't some silly phase? The best way they could truly *see* that passion, was as a lead.

The conversation paused while we got our food and headed for our usual table where Shay waited for us with her sack lunch.

"I'm sure it was fine. And besides, we're sophomores! We've got two more years to audition." Izzy picked up the conversation from where we left off. She put down her tray and waved at Cody as he walked by. She looked at me and grinned because she knew I was totally shipping them.

Tessa sighed as she sat down. "I don't know if I should accept a part if I get one. With State Finals in three weeks, it's going to put a lot on my plate." She put her napkin in her lap. "Maybe the baby will come when I'm away, so I won't have to deal with that either."

Tessa's dad was expecting a baby with his girlfriend, and the impending birth was making Tessa distracted and flustered, which was very unlike her. We had talked her into auditioning in spite of being super busy with swim team. It would give us more time together.

Izzy and Shay talked with Tessa about the baby dilemma. I should have joined in to encourage her, but I was distracted. I kept spinning ideas of how to convince Ms. Larkin to give me an audition do-over.

After lunch I made sure I was the first one in the door of the Drama 2 class. Ms. Larkin was writing a schedule on the board but smiled at me when I came up to her.

"Hello, Amelia."

I barely took a breath before diving right in. "I was hoping maybe you'd thought about it some more and maybe are willing to reconsider?" I held onto the straps of my backpack like it was a parachute holding me up as I drifted down from the sky. "I know you've made exceptions before when people are sick, so there's a precedent?"

The bell rang, and the door banged open as students started drifting in. I ignored them, keeping my eyes trained on Ms. Larkin. I felt her wavering, could see her face softening.

"I'm not trying to take advantage of anything, I promise. It was genuinely hard for me to audition without my soundtrack. I do admit it was my fault for misplacing my phone. Ms. Larkin, I would like the chance to do it for real—with my soundtrack as I had practiced. This is what I love. I won't be able to live with myself if I don't at least give it my best try."

I gripped the straps tighter and watched her place the cap back on the dry erase marker and lean on the whiteboard.

"Okay," she said.

"Okay? Really?" I squealed.

"One time. I'm not going to do this again. And we'll do it right here in this room after school before the second round of auditions begin. I'll have Mr. Thompson stop by so someone else is here. Is that agreeable?"

She didn't look very happy about acquiescing, but I didn't care. I nodded quickly. "Yes, yes, that's fine."

When I got to the carpet where Jenna, Presley, and Brie were sitting, I realized I would be singing in a bright room where I'd be able to see the faces of my small audience. Whatever. I couldn't worry about that because I had to try again no matter the circumstance.

The Trio gave me a bit of a surprised look when I sat down, but I grinned and said, "So, are you auditioning today?"

"Yep," Jenna said flatly.

"There was a good turnout yesterday. I bet Ms. Larkin is glad to have so many actors to choose from." I continued acting like I belonged there, sitting with them, the musical theater girls.

"Lots of room for ensemble in this show," Presley said. "And there's so much dancing! It's my dream to choreograph a show someday. Maybe she'll let me next year when we're seniors?"

"I don't see why not. You should tell her now, so she remembers you next year!" Brie said.

Jenna raised an eyebrow at me. "How did your audition go, Millie?"

I almost corrected her on my name but decided against it. I wasn't going to give her the satisfaction of ruffling me. "Fine." I turned back to Presley. "I bet you could ask to assist this year. Priya seems super nice. With such a large cast, I'm guessing she'll need a dance captain. Couldn't hurt to ask. You're the best dancer in the school."

Presley looked flattered and leaned toward me. "You think she'd let me?"

"You won't know unless you try. Come on, let's ask Ms. Larkin now." I stood and held my hand out to Presley and pulled her up. We walked over to where Ms. Larkin was doing something on her computer. I nudged Presley.

"Hey, Ms. Larkin. I was wondering if maybe I could assist the choreographer or be a dance captain for the show? I mean, I still want to be in it and all, but I would like to help with the choreography too," Presley said.

Ms. Larkin cocked her head. "I'll see what Priya says, but I'm sure we can use your help with dance. Everyone is going to be helping out in other areas no matter what their part."

"Okay! Thanks!" Presley said. She squeezed my arm as we headed back to our seats. "Thanks, Amelia!"

Score. One step closer to making The Trio a quartet.

Chapter
7

I DIDN'T TELL ANYONE about my second audition and obsessed about it the rest of the day. I grew more and more nervous as the clock ticked toward the final bell. And since I washed my hair that morning, my hair had become completely unruly. I tried, but failed, to blow-dry it the way Ava had. My attempts made it worse, so plopping a beanie on top was my only option to tame it. I guessed I'd be wearing a beanie until it got long enough to not stick straight out above my ears.

The good thing was, with a beanie, I looked like a more convincing Peter!

Today I would do what I needed to do. I had begged for another chance. I couldn't blow it this time. I auditioned once, so I could do it again. The worst was over. Because I was going to do it perfectly this time.

I jumped when the bell rang and went straight to the drama room where Ms. Larkin was waiting at the door.

"Let's do this quickly so I can get set up for the auditions." Her smile lacked its usual warmth.

I followed her inside and gave Mr. Thompson a small wave. He was sitting deeply in a big, soft chair, making him look very relaxed. He waved back. Ms. Larkin pulled her rolling desk chair near him and sat down, clipboard on her lap.

"Whenever you're ready."

Good. She didn't seem too irritated with me. Mr. Thompson looked like he'd rather take a nap.

I fumbled with my phone and opened the "I Cain't Say No" track. The song is about a confident girl who can't stop kissing boys. Like Peter, she is fun and sassy and full of personality.

I found a spot in the room to focus on—a large whitewashed wood sign with the word *Believe* written in script hanging on the wall behind them.

Believe.

Believe I could do this.

Believe I was already Peter.

I took a long, slow breath.

I sang as if I was on the big stage, telling a story to a giant audience. I melted into Ado Annie and her heartfelt explanation of her impulsive behavior. I *was* Ado Annie.

When I finished, I let my eyes drop to Mr. Thompson, and he was smiling. Ms. Larkin was wagging her head and looking . . . I wasn't sure. I couldn't quite place her expression.

Whatever it was, hope swelled inside of me.

Ms. Larkin stood up. "Feel better?"

I nodded. I did. I nailed it. Maybe it took me two tries, but I nailed it. I was so lost in the character that I was probably not a great judge of whether every single note was right—but I performed the heck out of it.

"All right, well, we have to get going." She turned to Mr. Thompson, who didn't look interested in getting up. "You ready?"

I grabbed my backpack while he was still extricating himself from the chair and hurried out, my thoughts spinning.

That had to be enough to get a callback.

I swung by the chaos of the auditioners waiting in the hallway and gave Izzy and Tessa a good-luck hug, then hurried to the parking lot where Mom was waiting.

I wasn't going to be able to relax now until I got that call.

—⁂—

The rest of the night I paced in my room, scrolling mindlessly through social media as I wore a path in the carpet. Texted in our Fan4 chat about Izzy's and Tessa's auditions—which both said were nerve-wracking but otherwise uneventful. Created six Insta posts about my dog. But my mind kept yanking me back to wondering whether my performance was "enough."

I thought about Ms. Larkin's face. She looked . . . amused, I decided. But that was good because the song was funny, and you're supposed to shake your head at this crazy, impulsive girl.

This afternoon I had done so much better than the first time. I knew that. But how did I stack up against everyone else? There was no way to know. I mentally ticked through everyone I knew who was auditioning, calculating who would be considered for which roles and whether there was room for me in any given scenario.

I'd heard dozens of messages at youth group over the years about not comparing yourself to others. But musical theater was a world where comparison was inevitable. This person sings better than that one. That person dances better than the other one. This one acts better than the one over there. And in musical theater, one person could be better at one thing but weaker in something else. The directors had to consider what was most important for the role. That was subjective too.

Add to that the truth that the actual talent of the actor wasn't enough—there was the "what you looked like" factor as well. Regardless of whether it was right or wrong, looks did matter.

I thought about Ainsley calling me fat.

She wasn't wrong.

I did a Peter Pan pose and looked at myself in my mirrored closet doors. *Yeah. I could be Peter Pan.* Peter didn't have to be a certain size. Mary Martin had set the tone for the onstage Peter— petite with a perfect pixie cut. Years later, Cathy Rigby played the role of Peter, and she was tinier than Mary. The images stuck. But did Peter have to be petite forever?

Truthfully, Peter was an *idea.* He was youth and exuberance and life. I could portray that. I knew I could. I only needed the chance to prove it.

From the beginning I knew my long hair wasn't right for the part. Nothing about it was like Cathy's or Mary's. So I cut it off, and it still wasn't right. I didn't feel like a Peter Pan. I just felt exposed somehow without all my hair.

My phone kept buzzing, so I lay on the floor and swiped through the texts, sending strings of emojis to the Fan4.

Part of me wished I had stayed for the auditions, seen who was there. Listened to the chatter. But that would have made me crazier. An irrational part of me wondered why I couldn't skip the next five hours and go straight to an email inviting me to callbacks.

I tried to work on homework. Did some research on Broadway stars and where they went to college. Looked at social media, watched several YouTube videos, then went downstairs to watch *Last Man Standing* reruns with Dad.

By eight o'clock I was starting to freak out. Auditions ended at seven thirty. I knew it was too early for decisions and emails, but my nerves wouldn't listen to reason. I texted the Fan4 and asked if they'd heard anything. That sparked a whole thread about how none of them were expecting a callback. Shay texted that she had told Ms. Larkin multiple times that under no circumstances was she to be put on the cast list.

I wished I had Presley's number. I could kill some time asking her about how she got started performing professionally. I checked The Trio's Insta and Stories and Snap for a post about a callback. Nothing.

The night dragged on. I repeatedly checked the social media of everyone who might get a callback. Kevon, the guy everyone thought would be Captain Hook, was the first to post on his Story "Callback, baby!" As if it was a surprise that he got one.

I refreshed my email. Nothing.

Every time I saw another callback announcement pop up, I checked my email. My heart sunk as more and more stories mentioned callbacks. I refreshed my email over and over, knowing they were probably sent out in batches.

By ten I was ready to cry. No email and way too many people celebrating their callbacks.

No callback meant no Peter.

Not even a chance.

I felt so many things. I was sad and angry, but more than that I felt like a fool for believing it could happen. What a great time for a Peter who looked like me, I had thought. This is what I thought God had planned for me. My belief in this single outcome had so fully consumed me that now I was incapable of understanding that Peter had vanished completely.

This had been my foolproof plan to prove to my parents that I was serious and could do this for a career. And now whatever part I got certainly wouldn't remotely help my plan.

I yanked a comb through my hair. My stupid hair. My act of faith.

Why would God do this to me? How could He make me believe I had the part and then take it away like that?

I crawled into bed and pulled the covers over my head.

I tried to talk Mom into letting me stay home from school, but not only did she refuse to entertain the idea, she also made me drive.

"You're not getting enough practice. You need many more hours before you can take your driving test."

I was not in the mood. Driving meant I actually had to concentrate. "Well, I'm never going to get enough hours driving the ten minutes to and from school!"

"Did you check your mirrors?" she asked.

"Yes." I tried not to let it sound nasty, but it definitely sounded grumpy.

I began to back up.

"Too far! Too far over!"

"I might hit Dad's car!"

"You're not going to hit it! Don't cut the wheel so much. Go straight, then turn the wheel once you get to the end."

I pressed my lips together and tried to go straight, but I still bumped the trash can on the way out. It stayed upright. This time.

"Why do you make me do this on trash day?"

"Check your mirrors again. People walk a lot at this hour."

"I know!"

The rest of the drive to school wasn't as bad as the driveway, but once I got there, I had to actually go inside the school and face people. My plan was to keep my head down, jet to my locker, and then rush to first period without any interaction with my friends or anyone else who would talk about the cast list. But there it was. Just like I'd remembered from last year after the cast had been announced. Buzz about the musical filled the hallways. Filtered into classes. There would be no escape from reminders of my failure. Again.

I tried to block it out without sticking my fingers in my ears and singing, "La, la, la, la." It sort of worked.

Then I walked into Drama 1.

Tessa, Izzy, and Shay looked over at me with identical expressions of compassion and pity. I wasn't in the mood to face or deal with their sympathy. I preferred to disappear. I knew they cared about me, but none of them understood, not really.

"It's fine," I said, slumping onto the purple beanbag chair.

"I'm sure you're disappointed," Shay said. "We're sorry."

Clearly they had talked about me. *Terrific.*

I shrugged. I planned to say something flippant, but the words caught in my throat. Instead of letting my voice crack, I swallowed them whole.

"None of us got a callback either," Izzy said. I didn't look at her.

I searched for Ms. Larkin, wishing she'd start class or give me some work to do so I could get away from my friends.

The girls started talking, hesitantly, avoiding the elephant in the room. Needing to ignore them, the class, and Ms. Larkin's predictable bright talk about *Peter*, I decided it was the perfect time to straighten up our small backstage area. When the end-of-class bell rang, I bolted without a word and went straight to the auditorium. Lunch in public, especially with the girls, was something I could not deal with.

The vast and empty auditorium filled me with an actual ache. I sat front row center, the ghost light throwing soft shadows across the stage. My heart was unable to fathom being absent from that stage this afternoon for callbacks. I couldn't imagine anyone wanting a lead more than I had. In the end, my passionate desire hadn't mattered.

A side door squeaked open. There was no point in ducking or hiding, exposed as I was in the center of the front row.

"Amelia?"

I sighed deeply. *Worst case scenario. Ms. Larkin.*

She walked down the stairs, her long skirt swinging.

I wasn't in the habit of being rude to adults. It was ingrained in me. But it didn't stop me this time. I was mad. And I deserved to be mad. "I don't want to talk."

"Is this yours?" Ms. Larkin held out my phone.

"Yes. Thank you," I muttered and took it from her, my cheeks flushing.

"May I sit?" She didn't wait for me to respond, lowering the seat to sit next to me.

Why did she ask if she was going to sit anyway?

I stared straight ahead.

"I know you're disappointed."

I clenched my teeth. I was not going to talk.

"Amelia. I appreciate your passion. I do. You have so much to offer the theater world. I'm excited to see where it will take you." She smoothed her skirt. "Theater is a tough world. Getting the part you want is a rare thing—it's more common not to get it. Remember what I've told you in class? An actor's first job is auditioning. Over and over and over again. Getting to perform up there? It's fabulous. But you'll audition a hundred times for every role you get."

I knew the statistics. But I didn't care. She had clout. She could have encouraged the others to make a different decision. She could have changed everything.

"A lot of different elements go into the decision process, and that includes who we invite for callbacks. Some drama teachers call back a ton of kids, but I think that gets everyone's hopes up for nothing. Here, we invite back only those we are seriously considering. I believe it's the kindest thing we can do, though I know it still hurts."

She was quiet for a few minutes. I stared at the puddle of light on the stage, willing her to leave. Arguing with her was pointless. But I had to know why. I broke my vow of silence.

"Why?" I choked out.

"Why what?" she asked.

"Why can't you see me?" I said. That was not the question I intended to ask. I meant "as Peter" or "as a lead," but once it was out of my mouth, I realized it was my question exactly.

"I do see you, Amelia. I see your heart. Your boldness. Your compassion. Your drive. Your willingness to work hard in whatever role or assignment you're given. It's impressive."

"If it's impressive, then why . . . ?"

Ms. Larkin paused a few beats before speaking. "First, we've talked about the 'look of the show' in class. Each director has a vision for what he or she wishes to create on the stage. Second, high school productions are handled differently than professional ones. Upperclassmen are given priority for the leads because freshmen and sophomores will have more opportunities for participation than those leaving the school first. You know that."

"I thought my audition was good," I said.

"It was. You've made so much progress from last year. Your vocals will continue to improve. One day there will be a show that has the perfect lead part for you. Because of your impressive theater qualities, I have been considering bringing you in for an important job. I haven't finalized what that will look like, but I'm hoping you'll consider it." She patted my hand. "We'll talk more, okay?" She stood up.

I didn't answer.

She waited a few moments, then turned and walked away.

Chapter
8

THE CAST LIST CAME OUT Sunday at 4 p.m. after a weekend of trying (and failing) to distract myself from thinking about it. Instead, I'd incessantly tortured myself.

I knew I wouldn't get a lead, and yet I still scrolled slowly through the list hoping desperately to see my name there. And it wasn't, of course. You don't get a lead without getting a callback.

Presley got Tiger Lily, and Jenna got Wendy. Presley had a great look for Tiger Lily. There were so many other girls who could have been Wendy, so it was an honor that Jenna got the part. I hoped she appreciated it.

I stared at Brie's name next to Peter Pan. Exactly as everyone had expected. Seeing her name in print was different than knowing it *could* happen. It was really over. All the wishing and wanting and believing and praying. Now it was real. And it felt so unfair. *Why had they bothered with auditions when long before, they had already decided Brie would be Peter?*

The three friends with the three female leads.

Maybe I should quit before finding my name. I didn't have a lead, and nothing but a lead mattered to me. Except for Presley and me, I didn't know anyone else in the school who wanted to do this as a profession. They were having fun on their way to some other career. I was serious about it. Dedicated. *Why couldn't Ms. Larkin take that into consideration?*

I was angry, yes. But what I felt rise up in me was more than anger. Next to the anger was fear. *What if her decision really meant I wasn't good enough?*

I scrolled through the other parts, searching for my name. Tessa and Izzy were both in the Lost Boys ensemble. But my name wasn't with theirs. *Why couldn't I at least be with them?* That might have been a little easier to bear.

And then. There it was. The Pirate ensemble.

She made me a *pirate*? I felt sick.

I turned off my phone screen. It started buzzing. I ignored it.

I didn't want to do the show anymore. Being a pirate wasn't going to get my parents to see anything at all. And if I didn't convince them that I needed professional training to get better at my art, then I'd be no better than an ensemble member for the rest of my life.

There had to be a different way.

I tapped on my phone and pulled up the three local community theaters I knew about. One of them was a small group that only did plays. I enjoyed plays, but they felt so small compared to the big musicals. Even on Broadway it was the musicals that drew the big crowds.

The two organizations that did musicals were Kids Theater International and Aspire Christian Theater. I had been to several shows at each, and they were generally good, but both groups were expensive to participate in. They required at least one parent to be involved as a volunteer, and mine, well, they already volunteered so much at church.

KTI's auditions for *James and the Giant Peach*—a show I wasn't very familiar with—had closed. But Aspire was having their *Wizard of Oz* auditions the next weekend. I signed up for a slot on Saturday.

I went downstairs and found Dad at the kitchen table in front of his laptop. I sat next to him. "Dad. I need to ask you something."

He looked tired, but he smiled, took off his glasses, and leaned back in the chair. He was soft in all the ways Mom was hard. Right now, he was sporting a deep five o'clock shadow. "Shoot."

"I'd like to audition for *Wizard of Oz* at Aspire, but I can't unless I take a class, so I am asking if you would please let me take this class. It's a vocal group, and I think it would help me a lot. And if you sign me up, I can audition for their big show on Saturday, and I really, really want to do it. Please?" I realized I might not be making total sense but hoped he'd get the gist.

"Aren't you doing something like that at your school?"

"I want to do this instead," I said. I showed him the information on my phone.

Dad slipped his glasses back on and squinted at my phone. He gave up and switched to his laptop. "What's the site?"

I got him to the page and waited while he read it.

He looked up. "Sorry, Mills. This looks like a Mom question."

"She's gonna say no."

"Not necessarily. Regardless, this is a decision for the three of us."

"But you're the dad. You can say yes."

"That's not how family works."

"Neither is Mom saying no to everything."

"I'm texting her to join us, okay?"

"Fine." I slumped in the chair and waited for Mom to emerge from her bedroom where she was probably watching *This Is Us*. Basically, the one thing she watched besides HGTV.

She gave me a funny look as she sat at the table.

Dad slid the laptop in front of her. "Mills wants to do this."

She scrolled a little but shook her head quickly. "It says here that there's a pretty steep fee and parents are required to volunteer."

"Yes. But you only have to volunteer for a few months. Obviously I can't do it without your help. Please? I really want to do it."

"You just auditioned for *Peter Pan*. I don't understand why you're bringing this up," Mom said.

"I don't want to do *Peter Pan*." I pointed at the laptop. "I want to do this one."

"But you already auditioned for *Peter Pan*, so you've already committed to that one." Mom squinted her eyes at me. "I'm confused, Millie. Did you get a part?"

"Sort of."

"What do you mean 'sort of'?"

"I'm in the background."

"So you're in the show? There's nothing wrong with being in the background. The school isn't asking for a bunch of extra help or money, are they?"

I looked at Dad, but as usual he was letting Mom share her opinion.

"I don't want to be one of twenty pirates. I want a real part. Can't you at least let me try?" I rubbed my face, my thoughts desperately trying to come up with something, anything that might sway her.

She gave Dad a look and sighed. "You are already committed to your school show. This is not up for debate."

"We haven't started though. It would be no big deal for me to drop out."

"And what if you end up as one of twenty munchkins in this one?"

"I'll do it. Their shows are better than ours."

Mom snorted. "They *should* be for the amount of money they're charging."

"It's a Christian theater. That should make you happy."

"That's not the point, Millie, and you know it. Character is about honoring your commitments."

"You don't understand. Are you ever going to let me do any theater besides at school?" My heart thumped wildly.

Mom held up her hand like I was being ridiculous. "Whoa. We are saying no to Aspire because you already said yes to your school show. Don't make it so dramatic."

"I'm not being dramatic!" I fought to keep from shouting. My frustration at what I'd lost was threatening to fly out in shouting anger.

"Amelia," Mom warned.

I looked at Dad for help. He leaned forward and rubbed his chin. "What's really going on here? Why do you want to quit *Peter Pan*?"

I subdued as much frustration as I could, counted to three, and then said, "I plan to make musical theater my career, and I feel like I'm already so far behind. I won't learn anything being a pirate. I need a bigger part."

"We may not know much about theater," Dad said, "but we do know about life. And we can promise you that's not true. You'll probably learn more about theater being a pirate than if you had a lead."

"You can't quit when things don't go your way," Mom added. "God never wastes anything we go through, so I know He has something for you to learn during this show."

I fumed. *God? God could have changed Ms. Larkin's mind.* Instead He was silent. It seemed God didn't plan to help me succeed in theater any more than my parents did.

Mom closed the laptop and exchanged a glance with Dad.

"I don't want to do this show," I grumbled. Being a pirate felt so demoralizing. And embarrassing. I wasn't musical theater royalty. I was a pathetic wannabe.

"You climbed aboard this pirate ship." Dad laughed at his own bad joke but tried to stop when he saw my sour expression. "Stay on the ship. See what God will do." He patted the laptop. "We can consider this other theater at some point."

"Promise? Like really promise? I really need . . . more."

"I promise. But following through on your commitments is important, especially when things don't look the way you envisioned them," Dad said, echoing Mom.

They weren't going to budge. I needed to get out of the conversation. "Can I be excused?"

"Sure," Dad said. "And we're sorry about it not working out. Truly."

Mom gave an obligatory nod.

I seriously doubted they could understand. I would be invisible up there onstage. A part of a horde. No one would even know I was there.

Felix followed me to my room and jumped on my bed. I curled up next to him and let myself cry. I was so sad. So utterly disappointed.

Why couldn't things work out for once?

I wanted Peter more than anything I had ever wanted in my whole life and proved it by sacrificing my hair and auditioning—twice!—only to end up as a nameless pirate. The lowest of the low. Even the Indian and Lost Boy ensembles had more to do than the pirates. Yeah, I not only got an ensemble, I got the worst ensemble.

I buried my face in Felix's soft coat. He groaned and moved away, rolling to his back with his belly exposed. I lay on my back next to him. The ache of sadness changing to a wash of embarrassment. *Was there a way to never show my face at school again? I'd forever be known as the fat girl who thought she could play the diminutive Peter Pan.*

My phone kept chiming the trill I'd assigned to the Fan4 text group. I scrolled quickly past the chat about the show leads and slowed down at Shay's comment—which actually elicited a small smile.

> Shay: I know she promised not to put my name on the cast list but I needed to see it for myself before I could relax!
> Izzy: 😂 😂 😂
> Tessa: Amelia? How are you doing??
> Izzy: Earth to Amelia?
> Shay: Has anyone heard from her?

I thought about responding, but I couldn't decide on whether to text the truth or a cover story. I didn't want to be fake with them and wasn't ready to be fully honest either.

That left one person I could pour my heart out to—my brother. I found a comfy spot on the floor and FaceTimed Josh to fill him in on everything. Including hating my part.

He twisted his lips as he thought about it. He always did that right before saying something important. I missed him so much. When he lived at home, he was always quick to give me a big hug or mess up my hair.

He took a long breath in and out. "Well, you know what you have to do."

"I do? No, I don't."

"You have to be the best doggone pirate you can be."

I grimaced. "Doggone?"

He shrugged and laughed.

"I don't want to be a pirate."

"Humble yourself before the Lord, and He will exalt you."

"You're going to quote Scripture at me? Really?"

He gave me his signature smile. "I know you don't want to hear that, but you know I'm right."

He turned to say something to Jessica. Thankfully she didn't pop in. When he turned back, he repeated, "Be a great pirate.

Isn't there a theater saying about there are no small parts or something?"

I leaned back against my bed and stuck my legs out in front of me. "There are no small parts, only parts with less stage time."

"That's the one! So don't be small."

Exactly what I had told the girls before our One Acts. I picked at a tiny piece of lint on the carpet, unable to come up with a response.

"Hey, sis. I gotta run. Jessica needs my help."

His image froze, and then he was gone.

I let my phone fall to the floor and thought about my brother's words.

Was I being small by grumbling about being a pirate?

Was I being prideful?

I hoped that wasn't true, but I had a sick feeling in my gut that it might be.

I crawled into bed without changing into my pajamas. Whether or not it was true, I still wished I could walk into school and quit the show. Even if I couldn't be in another one.

Chapter
9

MORNING BROUGHT a bruised heart, swollen eyes, and a headache. I glanced at my Fan4 texts, but the thread dropped when they realized I wasn't going to respond. None of them would understand how I was feeling. They were enjoying their favorite passions. Tessa had her swimming—and was going to State Finals. Izzy had her baking—and was getting more followers to her Insta every day. Shay had the horse barn—and the promise of a job there come summer.

This was my thing. My one big thing—and I had nothing to show for it except a mini part as a stupid pirate. But I had to stay on the boat, or there wouldn't be other shows.

I thought of Josh's words and his hurt the worst. Probably because I knew he was right. I likely would have said the same thing to someone else in my position. Honestly, I *had* said it before. But it was so much easier to say and believe it when you weren't the one in the down position.

Did I really believe what he said? That every part mattered? I didn't think so. If there were nineteen pirates instead of twenty, would anyone notice? Nope. One less pirate would not change the show.

If I was the best doggone pirate I could be, would that be enough to convince my parents to let me do more than the "once a year" school musical? They probably wouldn't even be able to tell which pirate I was.

I wouldn't have said it out loud, but I thought I deserved better because I worked hard. I was more committed than anyone.

And I was stuck being a pirate.

The entire school was buzzing about the cast list. Presley, Jenna, and Brie looked like little starlets being mobbed by adoring fans. I kept my head down until Drama, where Izzy, Tessa, and Shay were waiting for me on the shaggy blue carpet.

"So?" Izzy asked.

"It's so awesome you and Tessa get to be together," I said with a big smile. I'd bury my disappointment behind a facade and put my acting skills to use.

"Yeah," Tessa said, looking uncertain.

"The Lost Boys ensemble will be so much fun," I said as I dropped to the carpet next to Shay. "You'll have some really fun dances and scenes."

"Amelia?" I heard Ms. Larkin's voice behind me and swallowed hard. I wasn't sure I had the acting chops to talk to her.

I turned.

"Come here for a minute?"

I wanted to say no but obviously you don't do that when a teacher asks for you, so I gave her a quick nod and got up to follow her into the hallway.

"I had hoped to catch you before class, but the morning got away from me."

I pressed my lips together. Speaking was risky.

"I know you're disappointed. I can see it on your face."

"I'm great," I lied.

"Well," she said, smiling in a sympathetic way, "I am asking if you would agree to be the stage manager for the production. I know you'd rather be onstage, but I see lots of potential in you, Amelia, and there are many different kinds of roles in the theater world. It's good to explore and understand all the facets of a production—and being a stage manager gets you involved in every part of it. This is a great year for you to immerse yourself."

Ms. Larkin looked pleased to offer me this position. To me it felt like pity rather than some kind of honor. A consolation prize. I didn't want her pity. I wanted to know why she couldn't imagine me as Peter.

She laid a hand on my shoulder. "You don't have to decide now, but I'd love to have your help leading this show. I think you'd be great at it. We'll talk more, okay?"

I followed her back into the room.

Ms. Larkin spent the hour talking to the class about the show and creating committees so everyone could participate in making the show happen.

After class, Shay turned to me. "Are you really okay?"

"Sure. Great," I said.

Tessa raised an eyebrow.

"Let's go to lunch." I led the way so I didn't have to make small talk or maintain eye contact.

Lunch was anything but normal. Alex joined us, which was fine, but it changed our dynamic. Shay kept throwing me questioning looks, which I ignored. Izzy was trying to figure out something that happened to her IGTV, so she was on her phone googling tips.

I ate. I pouted. I marched obsessively through my thoughts trampling over old ground again and again. *What more could I have done? Besides getting the audition right the first time?*

It felt like one of those dreams where you feel frozen and you can't move in any direction no matter how hard you try.

Nothing in me was okay with being a nameless pirate. I was aware of how arrogant that was but couldn't seem to do anything to stop it. The right thing would be to be a pirate and embrace the stage manager role so I might have the chance to join Aspire or KTI.

But knowing the right thing to do didn't make it any easier to actually do it.

—⚬—

It was painful to go to Drama 2 and watch everyone fawn all over Brie, Presley, and Jenna and for them to act humble about it. Like they were shocked and oh so grateful. It made me want to throw up.

I forced myself to go over and congratulate them and felt like a fraud doing it. I wasn't happy for them, and I felt awful inside for feeling that way.

I plopped myself onto a beanbag across the room. From there I could watch Jenna's little group. Ever since school started, I had longed desperately to be part of that royal trio. Extremely popular before landing at the top of the cast, their roles in the show cemented their royal reputation, showering them with even greater accolades and attention. It was like they had won some major award. *Who declared them* the *musical theater people? Why not me? Why didn't my passion for theater get noticed?* I belonged in that kind of club far more than Jenna and Brie did. *Did missing out on the musical last year make that huge of a difference?*

It made me wonder, *how* was *I seen at this school?*

Was I just the fat, loud redhead—like I'd overheard people say?

Really, though, how would anyone know anything else about me if that's all I let them see? I didn't have a major social media presence. I followed many but was only followed by a few. Felix was probably on my Insta more than me.

As I watched everyone pour congratulations on The Trio and

listened to the squeals rising, I thought how when people earn a reputation, it sticks. Even if the reputation is undeserved. I thought about Izzy and the Dropbox photo ring. When it exploded, people assumed she had sent a nude selfie to Zac—no matter how many times she denied it.

The scandal had consumed the school and local community. Good reputations had been smeared or ruined. Thankfully the buzz around the audition this past week took temporary precedence over it. But the ongoing investigation wasn't over, creating a dark tension that stretched throughout the school. No one knew what to expect, who to trust or mistrust, and who might be the villains in this story.

In English Lit, we learned that in stories, heroes are made the same way as villains. The story begins, choices are made, and labels take over, whether they are inaccurate or unfair. It took far more effort to undo a wrong reputation than it took to create it.

I didn't want others writing my story—making me the fat, loud redhead. I wanted to write my own. Help others see me the way I wanted to be seen. But to *be* something different I was going to have to *do* something different. I had to change something.

I grumbled. *Wasn't that what I had been trying to do in landing the role of Peter?*

Ms. Larkin interrupted my thoughts as she quieted the class. "How many of you want Peter to actually fly?"

Cheers exploded around the room.

"To make Peter fly, we need $5,000 to bring in the specialty company that can make it happen. The school does not have the extra funds to give us. So if Peter is going to fly, we have to fundraise the entire amount."

Nearly everyone was excited, throwing out ideas—some of them rather outrageous. It was hard not to be stirred by their excitement. *Was I going to let my pride keep me from being a part of the energy surrounding the production?*

I let their voices fade and slipped back into "poor me" mode. The scope of failing to get a lead reached far beyond my now ruined plan to get my parents to fully *realize* that the dreams I have aren't foolish just because they don't understand them. It also meant that I would miss out on the many perks of being a lead. I wouldn't be a part of their exclusive "club" that included rehearsals for scenes that required only their presence, which led to special moments, insider events, jokes, and stories. I would be locked out of the music theater royalty.

Unless.

If I took the stage manager role, well, it would give me access to . . . everything. I'd have a measure of authority. I'd be involved with the entire production, not just the pirate bits. The blow of losing Peter might be lessened if I had some clout.

Although I was angry with Ms. Larkin, she had given me a way to come out of this as part of the production team, a leader, instead of a nameless pirate. I'd be able to show my parents how committed I was to this show. It would be a win. The best one I could hope for, given the cast list.

I was mad. But I wasn't stupid.

I was going to be the best doggone stage manager ever.

Chapter
10

ONCE I DECIDED to take the role, I immediately texted the girls.

> Me: Ms. Larkin asked me to be the stage manager! That's why I'm just ensemble because it's such a huge responsibility!

They showered me with congrats and lots of heart emojis.

I planned to never bring up my loss of Peter again, although every time I adjusted my beanie, I remembered. To keep the hurt away, I had to stay busy. Thankfully there would be a ton to do. I figured if I kept myself moving, then I didn't have to think about God not holding up His end of the bargain. I would concentrate on being a great stage manager. I would make this the best show possible. And maybe, just maybe, my commitment would convince my parents how serious I was about a career in theater.

During Drama 1 the following day, Ms. Larkin introduced me as the stage manager. A sense of pride washed through me. I felt powerful. The feelings stayed with me as Ms. Larkin asked everyone to create groups and then tasked them to come up with an idea for a fundraiser and a plan to execute it. The class grew noisy and active as people clumped together and started brainstorming fundraisers.

Ms. Larkin turned to me. "Some of your preshow focus will be advertising and helping get as many of these fundraisers off the ground as you can. During rehearsals, you'll keep the notes about blocking, props needed and locations, and any other details you see needing attention."

When she finished her instructions, I trotted over to Tessa, Izzy, and Shay, who were in the beanbag chair corner.

"Baking! Of course!" Izzy said. She was wearing leggings with cactuses, and I could only guess as to why she chose those. "We can sell our baked treats at school during lunch!"

"I don't know," Tessa said. "That's so much work for you. I don't know that I can help with the baking."

"Yeah. Just imagine," Shay said. "*Our* cupcakes. Sitting next to *your* cupcakes. It would look like an episode of *Nailed It!*"

"No, it won't!" Izzy said. We looked at her like she was crazy until she said, "I don't mind doing all the baking. Honestly!"

Tessa didn't look convinced but then said, "Well, I don't have any other ideas. At swim meets we raise money through concessions, which is pretty much the same as selling cupcakes."

"I've got nothing," Shay said, throwing her hands in the air. "I'm so sorry."

"I don't mind!" Izzy said.

Though the girls were right, that Izzy would end up doing the bulk of the work, I agreed it was a good idea. And Izzy was clearly excited about it. "There's plenty you can help with that doesn't involve decorating cupcakes," Izzy said as she swiped at her brow.

"If you guys can help me with the prep and the cleaning, that would be a huge help. I'll be able to bake so many more if I don't have to worry about that stuff!" Izzy nodded at each of us.

Everyone agreed, and she cheered.

We discussed logistics and decided to sell at lunch on Fridays but also take special request preorders. We picked Thursday to bake the treats, so everything would be fresh on Friday.

I checked in on the other groups and took notes on their fundraising plans.

Everyone was excited, and I felt better than I had since the cast list came out. I could do this. I still felt a stab when I thought about Peter, but I reminded myself to stay busy in the boat. I could get through this.

In Drama 2, we essentially did the same thing, continuing from the day before. After I checked on each group, I inserted myself into Jenna, Brie, and Presley's triangle—where they were mostly complaining about not being able to have their phones during class. "What fundraiser are you guys thinking of doing?" I asked.

"We should do a GoFundMe," Jenna said. "Simple."

"I think Ms. Larkin encourages us to really own the project," I said. "Not just ask for donations."

"But people would give us the money. We don't have to do so much unnecessary work," Presley said. "Besides, we have so much to do. Our parts are like the whole show."

"My classes are really hard this year too," Brie added.

"Oh, shut up, Brie," Jenna said. "You're like a genius. Do you even study?"

"My grades are good because I study nonstop! But we're gonna be at like, every rehearsal. I don't have time for a fundraiser," Brie said.

I sat there, stunned that they not only didn't want to help—but they also didn't seem to care.

"Don't you want to fly, Brie? Jenna? You don't want to awkwardly leap around onstage, do you? Flying will bring the magic," I said.

"Of course I want to fly. But I don't think we have to make it so complicated," Jenna said.

"Hold on," I said. I went to ask Ms. Larkin about the GoFundMe idea because I honestly didn't have any arguments as to why that wouldn't be the fastest and easiest way.

She was on her phone, so I waited for a few minutes nearby. When she turned to me, she looked really stressed. "Sorry about that. I hate answering my phone during school, but it was an emergency."

"Is everything okay?" I was still feeling salty toward her, but she looked so raw that I was genuinely concerned.

"Yes. How are the groups looking?"

I filled her in, then told her about Jenna's group.

Ms. Larkin placed her folded hands on the desk. "GoFundMe and similar sites are not allowed to be used per the school board. I'm sure there are multiple factors involved in exactly why it's not allowed, but every school group has to raise funds the old-fashioned way."

"Ah, okay. I'll tell them. You sure everything's okay?" I asked.

"Of course. Come see me after class though, all right?"

I told Jenna, Brie, and Presley the bad news. They spent the remaining ten minutes of class talking about how stupid the school board was instead of coming up with an idea.

I didn't get it. *Why wouldn't they make an effort to help when they were the ones who would benefit the most?*

The bell rang, and I waited for the room to empty before joining Ms. Larkin at her desk. "You asked to see me?"

"Yes. We need to keep this private."

I nodded, pleased she would trust me with whatever this was.

"Brie came to me . . . concerned . . . about her role. Essentially, she's not feeling very confident. I talked her into staying in the role because I know she has the potential to be an amazing Peter. I promised we'd support her in whatever way we needed, and I'd like you to help me with that."

I stilled. *I lost Peter to someone who didn't even want the part?* A dagger piercing through me couldn't have hurt more.

"How am I supposed to do that?" I choked out.

"Be available. Be flexible to jump in and help her if she needs it."

I left the room stunned. I hurried to my next class, but the sting lingered.

Chapter

11

FOR THE NEXT TWO DAYS, I stayed very busy. I created documents with fundraising information, the cast list and contact information, and the tentative rehearsal schedule. When I showed everything to Ms. Larkin, she gave an approving nod and permission to upload them to Google Classroom for everyone to access. Our first rehearsal on Wednesday was really a non-rehearsal as we learned about the set and what it would look like when it was complete. The first "real" rehearsals were long and painful. We read through the whole show. We sang through the whole show.

We didn't start anything interesting until the following week when we blocked the nursery scenes with the actors playing Peter, Wendy, Michael, John, and the parents, Mr. and Mrs. Darling. At first there was some debate about whether we should have a real dog play Nana or put someone in a dog suit. Everyone decided the dog suit was the only option since it would take a professionally trained dog to do the specific tasks required of Nana.

I was in charge of noting every detail of what happened onstage on my printed script that was kept in a thick white binder. I drew pictures of the stage and the actors' movements. I made notes about entrances and exits and where the actors stood for each line. I found myself far more meticulous about getting these details recordedthan I had ever been about anything else in my life.

When I wasn't taking notes, I was watching Brie and picturing myself playing her role. I thought of things that I would do differently. Since acting is subjective, I didn't necessarily think I would be better than Brie. Just different. But knowing she didn't want the role? That colored everything I saw her do.

I liked having a job at rehearsals, to be asked to do things that affected the whole show. Especially because being a pirate was truly horrendous. My role consisted mostly of grunting and growling. We were told to dance badly to silly songs, which made the whole thing even more embarrassing and awkward. The desire to quit nearly consumed me. "Oh, come on," said Miranda, a freshman who was very tall and broad in her shoulders *and* the only other girl pirate. "We can stick together. Make it fun."

I turned away so she wouldn't see me roll my eyes.

On Wednesday, we finished working on the tarantella, the lively pirate dance directed by Priya, and I came offstage to find Wilson waiting for me in the wings.

I liked Wilson. He was tall and skinny and had brown shaggy, curly hair that was a shade lighter than his skin. His hair fell into his eyes, so he was typically brushing curls off of his face or adjusting his glasses. He wore the standard tech guy uniform: black T-shirt, black jeans, and black shoes. He was the kind of guy who always lingered around the edges, ready to jump in to do whatever was needed without noticeably inserting himself. A year ahead of me, he was the go-to guy for the tech pieces of pretty much everything we did on the stage.

"I figured you'd find me before much longer!" I said, hoping he hadn't seen the embarrassing pirate display.

"Thought I'd get a jump on lighting since I have to schedule the lift to adjust them. Can you talk? Or do you need to . . ." He gestured at the stage.

"Nah. I'm good. Mostly dance today."

"Then, please, let's go to my office," he said with a bow.

He meant the light booth, of course. I followed him to the rear of the auditorium, glad to step back into the managing role.

We each took a swiveling office chair, and he reached for his own script binder. He folded his hands across his stomach, moving the chair back and forth slowly with his feet. "So how's it going?"

"Okay," I said. It was strange to see him like this. In the hallways, classroom, or backstage, he didn't talk much, kept his head down, and moved quickly from class to class. But here he looked relaxed and in charge.

"It can get a little stressful with the show, and I, uh, wanted you to know I'm here if you need anything," he said with an easy smile. "My booth is a safe space."

"Thanks," I said. "It's been good so far, but I know it's still early." I looked at him, and maybe it was because he was being so nice or that his booth did feel safe that I sat back and added, "To be honest, I do whatever Ms. Larkin tells me to. Other than that, I'm not sure what I'm doing half the time."

He laughed. He had a nice laugh.

"I think that's all you're supposed to be doing. Don't worry. I can help you learn the drill," he said. "Lights going off and on, stay in place, et cetera, et cetera. You'll get the hang of it."

"Good. As long as I'm here, I'd like to learn everything I can. How long have you been doing this?"

"A few years. This will be my third musical production here. I've teched other plays here and with a couple of other theaters in town."

"Which theaters?"

"All of them. Most people want to act so everyone always needs tech help."

"Aspire?" I asked.

"Yep. And KTI and there's a little one downtown—"

"Second Street Players?"

"Yep. Have you done anything with them?" he asked.

"No. I want to, but they're expensive."

"Yeah, I've heard. I think they have scholarships."

"I'm not sure I'd qualify for one."

"Ohhh," he said.

He waited, and I almost went on and told him more, but I was beginning to feel flustered. Like I was too relaxed. Too open. We'd had brief conversations in the past, but this one felt different.

He tapped his open notebook. "Let's walk through the show, and you let me know if there is anything I'm missing, okay?"

"Okay," I said. I scooted closer so I could see the spreadsheet he pulled from his binder.

First, we talked through the three main staging areas— Neverland, the nursery, and the pirate ship—to discuss how many lights we needed for each. Then he took me through the spread-sheet, which helped me understand his side of the schedule. The entire production was like a giant puzzle with all sorts of moving parts. I found myself asking questions about lights and mics. Wilson was glad to explain everything in as much detail as I asked for. I didn't realize how long we'd been there until Ms. Larkin stepped into the doorway of the booth.

"There you are. I need to talk to both of you," she said. "I'm going out of town this evening. Amelia, do you think you can run rehearsals tomorrow and Friday?"

"Sure," I said. Though I wasn't sure at all. "Everything okay?"

"Yes. I'll be back Monday. Wilson, could you please get me a list of items we need to order?"

Wilson adjusted his glasses and dug around in his brown leather messenger bag that was scratched, scarred, and pretty beat up. I mentally fixed a heart emoji to it. He removed another spreadsheet and handed it to her. "I have a digital file I can email you. I know we probably can't get everything, so I have listed the items in order of priority."

"Perfect. I've emailed you both the scenes to run through while I'm gone, so we'll be on track for when I return Monday. Thanks." She patted the door frame and left.

"Do you want to, umm, go to get a smoothie or something?" He closed the binder and settled it into his bag without making eye contact.

I froze. It was like I couldn't understand what he was asking. I didn't know what to say. "Oh, I umm, my mom's waiting for me. Probably. Already mad."

"Cool. Yeah. That's cool. Yeah. We should go then."

He threw his bag over his shoulder, and we parted ways. That was the end of the conversation—but not the end of me thinking about it.

During the ride home, dinner, and attempting to finish a few notecards for my research paper, I could think of nothing except— what was that invitation? *Was it anything? Was Wilson just being nice? Why didn't he look at me when he asked? What did that mean? Did he want to spend more time with me? Why did I feel so weird and awkward about it?*

I decided he was probably being nice. That was the word I would use to describe Wilson. Nice. A little nerdy. A little messy. Nice.

I tapped my purple fine-point marker pen on the unfinished top notecard and thought about high school relationships. Tessa and Alex were the couple I knew best right now. Before they got together, it was so hard for Tessa to admit she liked Alex even though it was so obvious to the rest of us that she did. She hesitated because the idea of a relationship with Alex was scary for her. Something that I was starting to understand. My face warmed.

Doodling little purple hearts and flowers on the notecard, I focused back on Tessa and Alex. Their relationship was so different from the others I saw. They weren't one of those couples who were clinging to each other and making out in the hallways. They liked being together but were equally fine hanging out with their own friends. There were also a lot of little things you could see if you were paying attention. The kindness that passed between them. The way Alex looked at her. Handed her something. Or put her first. I often wondered what it would be like to be treated so . . . sweetly.

Then there was the Izzy and Zac fiasco. Basically, their relationship had been the exact opposite of Tessa and Alex's. It started fast with Zac giving Izzy lots of attention. It looked great on the outside. I loved watching Izzy sparkle around him. So it was devastating when she discovered he faked the whole thing to trick her into sexting him. When she wouldn't, he photoshopped a pic of her and blasted Social with it. I hated that he had done that to her—adding her name and photo to the Dropbox folder—and I was still angry about it. I was glad Zac had been kicked out of school and was likely facing charges. I hoped they'd catch the other boys who were involved as well.

Boys were a difficult issue for me. I didn't talk about it with anyone. I'd gotten close to the girls, but I felt myself holding back from them at times. I didn't know why exactly. Maybe because I learned to be wary of kids when I was little. I got teased in elementary school for being bigger than other kids, but I wasn't called the *F* word until fourth grade when Jazlyn Roberts asked me, "Why are you so fat?" She said it on the playground. It was biting cold, and I wore a pink hat and a puffy pink coat that made me feel like a giant marshmallow puff.

I didn't cry until I got home.

The comments didn't stop when elementary school ended and middle school began. They actually got worse and continued through middle school.

In high school I started wearing clothes that made me stand out. It wasn't that I *was* confident, but dressing boldly made me *feel* confident. Like putting on a costume. I did love my clothes and retro style, but I didn't *want* to do it—I *needed* to. It gave me the strength to ignore the "Is that an earthquake?" comments. Or girls using the words "huge" and "giant" randomly in their suddenly loud conversations as I walked down the hall.

Boys had never been interested in me. It hadn't mattered much to me before. But it was starting to matter as people coupled up more frequently. Other girls, especially the popular ones, always seemed to have boyfriends. Like having a boyfriend was an expected part of the ritual of high school. A ritual I couldn't see that I'd ever participate in. I was glad Shay and Izzy didn't have boyfriends, so it was more normal in our group not to have one.

I debated texting the girls about what Wilson had said. I tapped out texts but then deleted them without sending them.

Wilson asked me to get a smoothie today.

We were doing Peter Pan *stuff and Wilson asked if I wanted to keep working over a smoothie.*

Who was I kidding? He just wanted to keep talking about the tech stuff. It probably had nothing to do with me. I tapped out a text and pressed Send.

Me: So weird! Was doing tech stuff with Wilson and he suggested smoothies. ☹☹

Izzy: Wilson? Like the mic guy?

Shay: Yes, the mic guy.

Tessa: Wait. He asked you out?

Me: No! We were working on Peter stuff. He wanted to finish.

Izzy: Sure he did rofl

Shay: He seems like a nice guy.

Tessa: Very nice! Amelia! That's awesome.

Me: Guys it was nothing. I said no anyway cause Mom was waiting.

Izzy: awww no!

Shay: Tell him you panicked because of your mom.

Tessa: You said no?

Me: I couldn't go! Besides it doesn't mean anything.

Izzy: You don't know that! Maybe he's in love with you!

Tessa: Izzy!

Izzy: Well he could be.

Shay: If he is then it was probably hard to ask you. You have to give him another chance.

Me: Hold up! I never said he liked me.

Tessa: You never know.

Izzy: And now you've rejected him.

Shay: If she tells him why maybe he'll ask her again?

Tessa: I did think I've seen him look at you. During the one act.

Izzy: Oh my gosh you guys would be so cute!

I rolled my eyes at the texts. Though I was pretty certain Wilson wasn't actually trying to ask me out, it felt really, really good that the girls thought it was possible.

Chapter
12

ONE THING WAS CLEAR. If Wilson was asking me out, I had rejected his attempt, and he might not have the courage to try again. That put me in the awkward position of needing to make him feel comfortable so he would give it another try—if that's what he had been doing.

I wasn't sure how I felt about him, but I didn't want him to think I wasn't open to being friends. Really, getting to know each other as friends sounded a lot safer than dating. Tessa and Alex had been friends for a long time before they dated, while Izzy didn't know Zac at all.

I meant to act normal when I saw Wilson at the beginning of rehearsal, but instead of being normal, I got super awkward and avoided him. I could blame the confusion on running rehearsal by myself, but really it was because I had no idea what to say to him.

Mrs. Copeland, the faculty member in charge, explained to

the cast that Ms. Larkin left instructions to run the Neverland and
nursery scenes, then turned the rehearsal over to me. As I stood to
take over, Tessa whispered in one ear, "You've got this," while Izzy
singsonged in a quiet voice, "I know the stage director, I know the
stage director."

"Hush!" I whispered back, trying to look professional while
suppressing a laugh.

Some of the actors were eager to do whatever I asked. Others
clumped together and distracted one another. It didn't help that I
felt off-balance and weird being in charge, so I was grateful for Izzy
and Tessa's continued encouragement in the form of thumbs-up,
waving, and grinning widely.

I became annoyed with Brie and Jenna because every time we
stopped for a minute, they disappeared. When they did it for the
third time, I went looking for them myself. I found them near the
band room looking at their phones, laughing.

"Guys. You have to stay onstage. We need to run your scenes,"
I said.

They exchanged a look that I couldn't read, and Jenna said,
"Oh my gosh. Brie and I were just saying what a great job you're
doing."

"Really?" Her comment threw me a little off guard. "Thanks."

Brie nodded. "Definitely. It seems like you're doing a lot for
Ms. Larkin."

"I guess."

"We should hang out sometime," Jenna said. "We might get
together later tonight."

"Yeah. We have to run lines. So many lines," Brie added, rolling her eyes.

"Oh, yeah. I could totally help you with that," I said. They
were looking at me differently. I felt included. But I still had a job
to do right now. "Can we go run the nursery scenes? Everyone's
waiting."

"Oh, of course! Sure!" they both said.

When we got back to the stage, the set had been changed from Neverland to nursery.

Izzy and Tessa were waiting for me, released since their scenes were over for the day.

"We're going to my house. You come when you're finished, okay?" Izzy said. "Shay's coming when she's done with tech."

"Oh . . . I, um. I'm not sure I can come," I said. I glanced over at Brie and Jenna who were still talking and laughing.

"It's our first big baking night," Tessa said.

"I know. I have Peter stuff though."

They both looked disappointed.

"I have to get this rehearsal going. I'm sorry." I turned back to the stage and said, "Places for scene five!"

We had thirty minutes left to run ten minutes' worth of script, but we got nothing done. Everyone kept stopping and talking. I repeatedly asked for quiet. We'd get through a few lines, and then someone would need a line and everyone else started talking. No one cared that I was in charge. Mrs. Copeland was back in a corner reading a book, clearly not paying attention to the rehearsal. I finally gave up and told everyone to go home.

I went over to where Brie and Jenna were getting their backpacks. "So what time were you thinking of getting together?" I was hoping Mom wouldn't balk about taking me back out.

"Oh." Jenna looked startled and distracted. "Oh yeah, we'll text you. We're not sure yet. Presley has dance tonight."

"Do you have my number?" I asked.

"Yeah, it's on the Google cast sheet, isn't it?" Brie asked.

"Yep," I nodded.

Jenna threw her hair over her shoulder. "See you later!"

And both walked off.

I was excited. Hanging out with them, posting on Insta about running lines? That would be perfect.

I was getting my backpack and coat and shutting off lights when I turned and ran straight into Wilson. I screamed.

"Hey, it's me!" he said. "Sorry!"

"Oh! I didn't see you. You're standing in the pitch black. You scared me!" The words tumbled out.

"Let's go in the hallway," he said. "It's quite a bit brighter out there. You getting picked up?" he asked as we moved to the hall.

I nodded.

"Okay—we can talk on the way out." We began to walk from the back of the school where the drama department was located to the front where parents waited in the pick-up loop.

"You know, I can give you a ride home from rehearsals."

"Oh, yeah? I um, maybe? I can ask my mom." I cringed. I sounded like a six-year-old asking Mommy for permission. But I actually had to. She was weird about teen drivers. Including me.

"Okay. How'd rehearsal go?"

I relaxed a little. He seemed to be acting normal, so maybe I could too.

"Kind of a disaster," I said honestly. He didn't say anything, so I continued to fill the silence. "We got through some of Ms. Larkin's task list, but only a few people seemed to be taking it seriously."

"It's not you. It's like this every year. A lot of them are just in it to socialize. They're not thinking about the show."

"I don't get it. Why did they try out then? They're lucky to have been chosen. Why wouldn't they want it to be the best show possible?"

Wilson laughed. "You'd think that, wouldn't you? I think a lot of them try out to do something fun with their friends. Or because it's part of the high school experience. They aren't thinking about making a quality show. Since it's not something they plan to do for a living, they aren't giving it much effort."

"I want to," I said.

"Want to . . . ?"

"Do it for a living."

"Direct?"

"No. I don't know. Maybe. I know I want to be onstage. But I've never had the chance to be in one of the big productions, only the really small ones."

"You will. Hang in there." He bumped my shoulder and smiled.

Mom's CR-V was idling in the loop.

"Let's go over the timeline tomorrow. I think it might help you," he said.

"Yes. Yes, we need to do that."

"Don't you TA for Ms. Larkin? Fourth period?"

I nodded.

"Come to the auditorium tomorrow instead, and we can chat. Sound good?"

"Sure. Okay." I gave him an awkward wave before sliding into the passenger seat.

Mom was looking at Wilson.

"Drive, Mom, please. Drive. Now. Put the car in drive."

"Who is that?"

"Nobody. Please let's go." My mortification was heightening by the second.

"You should drive home," she said. She unbuckled, climbed out of the car, came to my side, and opened the door.

"Are you trying to kill me?" I hissed.

She shrugged. "You need hours."

There was no point in arguing. I walked briskly around the front of the car and did not look in Wilson's direction.

"This is going to give me a grand total of ten minutes," I muttered as I adjusted the mirror.

I drove home, distracted enough by the actual driving to not say anything to my mother until we pulled into the driveway.

"Would it help you if I could catch a ride home from rehearsals?" I closed the car door, trying not to slam it.

"With that boy?"

"Maybe. I don't know. There's lots of cast members who drive."
I moved up the walk toward the house with her behind me.

"What kind of driver is he?" she asked.

"I don't know. I've never been in a car with him." I tried desperately to rein in the snark. "It's only two miles."

"Statistically most accidents happen close to home."

I had the urge to bang my head on the wall.

"Well, it can't be fun shuttling me around. I need a ride tonight
too. A friend has a thing."

"Thanks for the specifics. What friend? What thing? When?"

"A few people from the cast want to run lines." I hated that I
sounded annoyed. I had to keep my tone under control if I hoped
to get a ride. I glanced at my phone. No texts.

"What time?" she asked.

Why did she annoy me so much? "I don't know." I had to get up
to my room. I was drowning in a pool of emotions that I couldn't
begin to sort out. "I've got homework."

"Okay. Let me know," she called after me.

I made it to my room and tossed my backpack in the corner.
I flopped back on my bed and scrolled through Instagram and
Snapchat and watched my phone for texts.

Izzy and Tessa both posted about the baking night. Tessa posted
a pic of herself with flour on her face. Izzy posted one of a perfect
cupcake in her outstretched hands. Since Shay didn't like to appear
on social media, she was always the designated picture taker.

They looked like they were having fun. It probably wasn't too
late to join them. But I wasn't up to faking a good time or acting
like everything was cool.

I really did have homework to do, so I pulled it out in an
attempt to distract myself.

It didn't work.

I waited for Jenna and Brie to text. They were probably waiting for Presley to finish dance. I could get their numbers from the cast list and text them first, but I didn't want to look completely desperate, though that was an accurate description.

I had been looking for a chance to talk to Presley about her musical theater experiences. Maybe she'd have some good advice. I also wanted to dissect the Wilson conversation with someone. And I could have if I had gone and baked—like I should have.

Instead I spent the whole night in my room. Alone.

Chapter
13

THE NEXT MORNING, I pushed aside the reality that I had ditched my friends—for nothing. Stupid. I absolutely did not want to face them. Little did Wilson know he would save me that embarrassment by asking me to meet with him during fourth period Drama 1.

I picked one of my favorite, simple outfits that wouldn't make me look like I was trying too hard—black ripped jeans, a vintage Rolling Stones T-shirt, and a bright, striped cardigan that hung down to my knees.

I went to the hall bath to brush my teeth and fix my hair. I hated looking in the mirror. And it wasn't that my hair was, basically, not very attractive. I was getting used to the new me—and the beanie helped. The bigger problem was that every day my foolishly chopped-off hair was a harsh reminder that God hadn't answered my prayer. I wasn't sure where I stood with Him. I was confused and hurting deep inside. *Where had I gone wrong? Had I missed something I was supposed to do?* If He cared about me, surely I would have gotten a better part than a pirate.

I checked in with Ms. Larkin's sub at the beginning of fourth period before I went to the auditorium and found Wilson in the light booth.

He was all business. He went through the tech timeline in exhausting detail. It helped to see everything laid out. But I was still nervous about how the parts of the show would pull together. The production was weeks away, but it didn't seem like we'd have enough time to set the lights and get the timing and focus right. "Wow," I breathed.

Wilson laughed. "Somehow it all gets done."

"I don't see how," I said. I pointed at the calendar. "So here's when we need to finalize blocking so you can finish the lights in time. Well, thank goodness that will be Ms. Larkin's job!"

"Yeah. I thought it would help you to see the big picture. You should check in with Mr. Van Hulzen about the sets. He's pretty good about having the bare bones ready. The painting and decorating will take some time, and the cast usually does that."

"Okay," I said.

"How's the fundraising going? For the flying?"

"It got off to a slow start, but I think the approvals are finally in. I'm hoping for the best. I started a hashtag for the show and the fundraiser! Look!"

I pulled up Instagram and showed him the #HelpPeterFly hashtag. Izzy had posted a cupcake photo. Chad's group was doing yard work, so they posted a funny pic around a lawn mower pretending they were flying. There was the obligatory car wash photo with everyone covered in suds. We scrolled through a few other posts.

"You did all that?"

I shrugged. "They're doing the work, and I'm trying to get it organized on social media. *The Riverbend News* posted about it!" I showed him the repost pic. "I started an Instagram account for Northside so we can promote the show with #NorthsidePeterPan. Can you believe they didn't have one? It's @NorthsideHighTheater. Can you follow it? It's never too early to get the word out."

"You're good at this marketing thing." He laughed as he tapped his phone a few times, and then he looked up at me. "Followed!"

The bell rang for lunch, and since I had no idea what else to say, I said, "I should go meet my friends for lunch."

"Okay. See you later."

As I walked away, I realized I should have asked what he was doing for lunch. *Did girls do that?* I was so clueless, I really didn't know. I didn't even know which lunch period he had.

I grabbed a burger and fries at the cafeteria, then went over to where the girls sat at a long table covered with a pink table-cloth, a giant cupcake centerpiece, and three different flavors of cupcakes—strawberry, chocolate, and vanilla. Perfectly decorated, they looked like they came from a high-end bakery.

"You okay?" Shay asked as I set my tray down next to her.

"Just a meeting about the show." I fished my phone out of my pocket and announced to the others, "These look amazing!" I moved around the table taking a bunch of pics. "Delicious."

Tessa pointed at Izzy. "All her."

Izzy grinned. "You guys helped a ton!"

"We missed you last night," Shay said.

"Yeah. I know. I'm sorry." I dropped my phone back into my pocket and picked up my napkin.

"What was so critical?" Tessa asked.

Fortunately, a few customers came up at that moment. Word spread quickly about the yummy cupcakes, and the line stayed steady throughout lunch.

In between bites of burger, I edited a couple of the cupcake photos I'd taken and posted them with our #HelpPeterFly hashtag on both my account and Northside High's. When I was done, I took my turn selling, glad Tessa didn't reiterate her question.

When lunch was over, we packed up and went our separate ways. I was relieved. There had been tension for sure, but lunch went better than I expected. Maybe the tension would blow over on its own.

In Drama 2, I joined Brie, Jenna, and Presley in our fundraising group like nothing happened. They didn't mention anything about not bothering to text me. And they still had no fundraising plan.

"It took the other groups a while to get approval, so you should probably pick something," I said. "Today."

"Let's make it easy and do the car wash?" Presley said.

"Don't you think it's still too cold?" Brie said.

"We can't wait much longer," I said. "We need the full $5,000 before the company will commit."

The three of them looked around the room, looked at each other, looked at their phones.

"What were your other ideas?" I tried.

"The GoFundMe," Jenna said.

I pressed my lips together and tried to suppress the crazy I felt creeping into my eyes. "Well. That's not an option, so maybe we come up with other ideas?"

Brie folded her legs under her and stared at her phone. Then she laughed. "We could do a kissing booth!"

"Eww. Can you imagine the horrible people who would sign up?" Presley said. "Gross."

"Fine. At least do the car wash. What date were you thinking?" I said, trying to get the conversation back on track.

"Can't do it this weekend. Next?" Brie asked.

"I'm going to my grandmother's in Cincinnati," Jenna said.

"I've got rehearsal with another show," Presley said.

"Then the Saturday after that?" I went over and grabbed my phone from the organizer. I sat back down.

"Maybe," Jenna said.

Presley shrugged. Brie frowned.

"Saturday after next." I put the date in the Google Doc paperwork while they sat there and did nothing. "You'll have to ask a business for permission to do the car wash on their property. Any ideas?"

Crickets.

"I know the Dunkin' on 54 has hosted car washes. Maybe that one?" I asked.

"That's fine," Brie said, not looking up from a textbook.

I wrote it in, then said, "Who will ask the Dunkin' if that date is okay?"

Crickets.

"Well, I can't do it! I don't drive!" I snapped.

"You don't have to get snarky. No one asked you to go," Presley said.

I had to leave before I said something I really regretted.

—⁓—

That afternoon, although I had scheduled to rehearse the Neverland scenes, the stage was set for the nursery, so I decided to run those first—which would have been great, except Jenna and Brie were nowhere to be found. I double-checked the conflict sheet, and since they hadn't recorded any conflicts, I started without them.

I looked for replacements and saw Izzy and Tessa sitting with the others from the Lost Boys' ensemble in the auditorium. "Izzy! Can you come read Wendy?"

Izzy squealed, crawled over Tessa, and ran up onto the stage. I pointed at a pile of scripts. "Page 12," I said.

As for Peter? I would read Peter, doggone it. Since we had practiced the nursery scenes more than the others, I didn't need a script. I knew it cold. I threw myself wholeheartedly into becoming Peter.

And in the spot where Brie cartwheeled, I did one too. It wasn't as pretty and delicate as hers, but mine earned me a very surprised reaction and applause from the random cast members who were paying attention.

I guess they thought fat girls couldn't cartwheel.

My heart soared playing this part—this part I was meant for. And I held onto every moment like a treasure. Izzy did a pretty good job as Wendy. She was enjoying her momentary role almost as much as I was enjoying mine.

After we finished the scenes, I called to the stagehands to switch out the scenery, so we could move on to Neverland. As Shay and the others exchanged the sets, I noticed Brie and Jenna standing by the curtain, arms folded, scowling at me.

I refused to be intimidated. They hadn't been here at call time. It was their choice to miss rehearsal. Although the play revolved around their characters, we could not continue to let them hijack rehearsals with their absence.

Ignoring them, I helped the stagehands get the giant mountain positioned correctly on its mark. Well, it wasn't a mountain quite yet. So far all we had was the sixteen-foot-long platform and rough frame that would become the mountain, along with two sets of stairs for the actors to make their entrances.

"Actors in your places!"

The Lost Boys surrounded Peter onstage and giggled their way through "I Won't Grow Up." Priya directed the dance without once getting frustrated at the cast members who went right when they should have gone left, stood when they should have moved. By the third time through, it was looking pretty good. Such a cute dance. It made me wish, once again, that I was a part of this ensemble rather than a pirate.

"Before we move on," Jenna said as she stepped forward, "I would like us to take a moment to discuss the end of this dance. My movements don't make sense."

Priya gave her a funny look.

"We can talk about that later," I said. "We need to—"

"I think we should do it now," Jenna interrupted. "While Priya is here." She had a small smirk on her face, her eyes looked sharp, and her posture was very "try me."

I wasn't going into a standoff with Jenna Ashcroft. She was derailing us on purpose. I wasn't going to engage, nor could I stop the whole rehearsal to rework the dance—especially since it was unnecessary, and it only involved her. "We have to move on," I said.

Jenna turned to Priya. "Can we do it again, and I'll show you what I'm talking about?"

Priya said, "We can go backstage and discuss it."

Jenna glared at me as she went offstage with Priya. For the first time, I saw in her eyes what Izzy described from the locker room confrontation when they'd bullied her—with a hideous bra, of all things. I wanted to punch her. I had fifty people waiting for us to continue. Sort of. Most were busy talking and wandering. I tried to get the train back on the tracks, but we never quite got there. Every time we stopped to correct something or ended a scene, off the tracks we'd go again, and I would have to repeatedly ask for everyone to focus and get started all over again. It took five times as long as it should have. As a result, there were three scenes on the rehearsal list that we never got to.

By the time I excused the final actors, I was exhausted. Izzy and Tessa had gone home sometime in the previous hour. Shay's aunt had picked her up for a dentist appointment. As I began to gather my things, Wilson sauntered over. "Can I give you a ride?"

"Mom's picking me up today. I'm trying to get permission to ride home with you, but everything with my mother is more complicated than it needs to be."

"Do I need to give her permission for a background check and provide a urine sample?"

"Good idea. That might work," I said, my attempt at a joking tone falling flat.

"You okay?" he asked.

"Not really. I don't know what's wrong with everyone."

"What do you mean? From the catwalks it looked like a normal rehearsal to me."

"Is it?" I waved my hand at the stage behind me. "Because it seems like everyone's irritated. I mean, not everyone, but the vibe, you know? Something's off, and I don't know how to fix it."

"Well, yeah. I would say the vibe is off." Wilson shifted his feet and shoved his hands in his pockets. "If it's caused by what I think it is, it might get worse."

"What do you mean?"

He handed me a crumpled half sheet of green paper, printed to look like a flyer—which meant there were probably a lot more like this one. "I was going to throw it away, but then I thought you should see what's going around. And I'm guessing Ms. Larkin will want to see it when she gets back."

"Peter Pan features The Dropbox Girls"

Jenna Ashcroft

Fatima Jameel

Corinna Randall

Selena Maldonado

Dee Ikner

Izzy Valadez

My heart sank, and I felt sick. "Where was this?"

"Guys' bathroom."

"Well, thank goodness it wasn't posted on Social like Izzy's doctored photo was."

"Whoever did this probably did it because a digital source is a lot easier to trace than a paper one."

He was right, of course. "Did you show this to Mrs. Ventrella?"

He shook his head. "Not yet. After I discovered it, I tried to find as many flyers as I could and throw them away before any more of them got out. I wasn't quick enough—there's already a lot of chatter about it."

Like I needed something else difficult to deal with. "Thanks for telling me, Wilson. I'm going to see what I can do."

As I walked the near-empty halls, hoping the principal was still in her office, I texted Mom and said I'd be out after I took care of a little emergency.

The front office was empty and dark, but Mrs. Ventrella's light was on, so I knocked on the doorjamb and stepped into her open doorway.

Mrs. Ventrella looked up from her paperwork, her smile warm and her voice kind. "Miss Bryan. How are you?"

I set the flyer in front of her. In one big rush of words, I explained where it came from.

Mrs. Ventrella nodded as I spoke. When I finished, she tapped the paper. "Someone else brought one in earlier. Deputy Packard and the other officers involved with the case have been informed."

"But how did they get those girls' names? Except for Izzy's, of course. Aren't their identities supposed to be private?"

"Yes. We are doing what we can to keep the identities of everyone involved confidential. However, any male student who accessed that Dropbox account would be able to share names." She tucked the paper into a file folder lying on her desk. "Unfortunately, there is no way to trace it. We can assume it was one of the male students we've interviewed or who has been implicated, but there's no way to know."

"There's nothing we can do?" I felt another wave of nausea.

"I wish there was, truly. Unless someone comes forward with

firsthand knowledge, I'm afraid not." Mrs. Ventrella wore an expression of sadness and frustration. "I promise you that isn't going to stop us from asking students about it. In fact, Deputy Packard has already pulled the likely culprits. But without proof, all he can do is question and caution."

Chapter

14

It took some coordination and a lot of texts, but I managed to get the Fan4 to the bookstore to share the bad news. Dad dropped me off near the bookstore. It was a beautiful early spring night, and many of the nearby restaurant patios were full of customers. I opened the door to Booked Up, the bell tinkling. Shay's Aunt Laura greeted me and gestured toward our normal spot.

I found Izzy, Tessa, and Shay already gathered in our little alcove, worried expressions on their faces.

I simply handed them my phone with a snapshot of the flyer. They huddled over it, reading. Izzy covered her face with her hands. When Tessa and Shay looked up, I filled them in on my conversations with Wilson and Mrs. Ventrella.

Tessa flopped back on the love seat, looking overwhelmed. "Who would do this?" Tessa asked. "This is completely despicable." And then she put her hands over her face and burst into tears.

"Tessa?" Shay said.

"Oh, Tessa!" Izzy took her hands away from her face and grabbed Tessa in a big hug. "What's wrong?"

When Tessa could speak again, she said, "To make this little get together even more fun, Rebecca's in labor."

"Wow," Shay said.

"Isn't it early?" Izzy asked.

Tessa nodded, wiping her cheeks.

Shay wagged her head. "A baby should be happy news, but . . ." She drifted off because we knew exactly what she meant. Tessa's new half sibling added a new and complicated dimension to the fallout of her parents' divorce.

We sat there, speechless. *What do you say about something so hard? So conflicting?*

After a moment Izzy said, "I'm sorry I don't know what to say. But we can pray for you."

Tessa gave a nod, a tear running down her cheek.

I bowed my head but didn't add my prayer to the others. The nagging voice inside said that my prayers were pretty worthless anyway. Maybe Izzy's prayers for a good person like Tessa would be different.

"Okay," Tessa said, swiping her cheeks and then slapping her hands to her thighs. "Enough about me. I mean. This flyer. Awful."

"It's truly horrible. Who would do this?" Shay scowled. "They should be punished for it."

Izzy ran her hands over her doughnut leggings. "Probably not going to happen. Look at how hard it was to get any proof about the Dropbox thing to begin with!"

Izzy was right. It took a complicated plan that included me swiping Zac's phone to get Deputy Packard actionable proof. The investigation and charges were currently focused on the ringleaders. So far Zac was the only one named. Word was getting around about the other boys involved in collecting photos and running the site. There was also gossip about the girls involved, but this paper felt very targeted and specific. Not vague and random.

"It's so unfair that the girls were outed but not the guys," Shay said.

"People still believe that was a real photo of me." Izzy put her face in her hands.

"Only people who don't know you," Tessa said. "I'm sure the same thing happened to other girls."

"Can you imagine if I sent him a nude picture on purpose? I bet girls who did send one of these guys a nude would be feeling pretty bad about themselves right now."

"I thought the tension during rehearsals was because Ms. Larkin isn't here. But maybe it's been this?" I said.

"There's been a lot of tension in the school and community ever since this came out," Tessa said. "I hear stuff at swim practice and meets. People are polarizing. Some people shrug it off like it's just teen stuff. Others push for someone to pay even if there's no proof."

"Truthfully, the guys who subscribed to that Dropbox should be punished," Shay said. "They're just as guilty. If they didn't pay to subscribe, the whole idea wouldn't have worked."

"I sure hope no one in the cast did this," I said, waving my phone as though it was the flyer itself.

My friends stared at the phone looking concerned.

"What if it is?" Izzy asked.

"Well, for one thing, what we can do is stand up for the girls," Shay said. "Speak up if we hear the cast or crew say anything."

"We can pray for the girls," Tessa said. "And for Amelia and the faculty."

Izzy and Shay nodded.

"Thanks," I said. "I'll take all the support I can get. And any eyes and ears on what's going on that I can't see."

Shay held up her palm, and I high-fived her.

We agreed there was nothing we could do about the culprits. We could really only care for the girls on the list.

"You know," I said, clapping once, "if all we can do is encourage the girls, then let's *really* encourage them. Like bombard them with encouragement."

"Encouragement attack!" Izzy laughed. "Overcome evil with good! I love it."

"We could stick Post-it Notes on their lockers," Shay suggested.

"Or stick the notes inside?" Tessa said.

"And say things to them in person, too. Let's do it! Make it clear that they are not alone."

Jenna came to mind. Maybe this is why she had been extra mean lately. I wondered how I could help her. "Why don't we each take a name on the list? That way we can be sure everyone is getting encouragement."

"Perfect!" Izzy shrieked.

Shay looked a little uncomfortable but took Fatima. I took Jenna, Tessa chose Corinna (who was on the school swim team), and Izzy took both Selena and Dee. We didn't care whether the girls had willingly participated or not—they needed someone to come alongside them.

All weekend I worried that the source of the flyer was a member of the cast. I reassured myself that everything would get back to normal once Ms. Larkin returned. She'd get the show on track, *Peter Pan* would be great, and in the process, my parents would see my commitment to musical theater. Over the weekend I also replayed on endless loop the glorious fifteen minutes I got to play Peter. Yeah, I would have been a great Peter.

But Monday didn't bring Ms. Larkin. Instead it brought an

early morning email from her. She said she needed to be away a few more days. I felt sick to my stomach.

I got Mom to take me to school early again, and I went straight to Mrs. Copeland's room. She listened as I explained the flyer, then said, "I don't know what you're asking me to do."

"You have to talk to the cast and tell whoever did this to stop." I hitched up my backpack.

Mrs. Copeland took off her reading glasses. "You have spoken with Mrs. Ventrella?"

I gave her a nod. "But—"

She put her hand up. "We need to leave this in the hands of the administration."

Instead of arguing, I went to Mrs. Rinaldi's room and made the same plea. Mrs. Rinaldi taught and conducted the pit orchestra so that we had live music to sing along with instead of a canned track. She shook her head. "I'm not touching this with a ten-foot pole."

"We can't just ignore it," I said.

"What do you hope to accomplish by addressing this issue? These girls will be even more mortified, and whoever is responsible clearly doesn't care."

I sighed. "Still. Shouldn't we do something?"

"Let's see what Ms. Larkin says when she gets back and speaks with Mrs. Ventrella. But it will blow over . . . eventually. These things always do."

I was frustrated and helpless. I didn't agree that it would blow over for the girls on that list. *But if the adults refused to address it, what could I do?*

During Drama 1, I stayed busy checking in with each fund-raising group and gathering photos to post on the school account.

Izzy, Shay, and Tessa launched Operation Encouragement by doing something for each girl. Izzy, of course, made special cupcakes for her girls and delivered them to their homes. Shay wrapped up a daily encouragement calendar for Fatima, and Tessa bought lunch for Corinna and ate with her. I gave Jenna a really cool card with a black-and-white photo of the Eiffel Tower and a little notebook to match. She didn't even let on that she'd gotten it.

Though I hadn't heard anything from Jenna, it occurred to me that some kind of encouragement might boost the morale of the entire cast.

—⚏—

At lunch, an excited Izzy couldn't stop asking Tessa questions about her baby brother born the night before. "Did you get to hold him?"

Tessa nodded. She speared a cantaloupe chunk and stuck it in her mouth, chewing as she stared at her bowl of fruit.

"Come on, Tessa! Spill!"

She looked up. Sighed. "He weighed seven pounds, six ounces. He's twenty inches long. Labor was somewhere around twenty hours. They named him Logan. Mother and baby are doing fine."

She sounded like a robot, but Izzy didn't seem to notice.

"Why did they name him Logan? Is he cute?"

Tessa set her fork down, fished her phone from her backpack, entered the security code, and handed it to Izzy.

Izzy practically shrieked. She wiped her hands on her napkin and snatched the phone. She swiped through a bit, and her face fell. "Where are the pictures?"

"Don't have any," Tessa said. She took the phone and put it back in her pack.

Shay touched Izzy's arm. "Maybe it's not a good time to talk about the baby."

Izzy huffed. "Fine." She slouched and dug into her burger once more.

"Izzy," Tessa said. "I'm sorry. I haven't sorted it out yet. I'm not sure what I feel."

Then Shay surprised me when she turned and said, "What about you?"

"What about me?" I asked.

"How are you?"

I was on the same wavelength as Tessa: let's not talk about the uncomfortable stuff. So instead of diving into my own muddled thoughts and feelings about Peter and the show, I filled them in on how neither Mrs. Copeland nor Mrs. Rinaldi would address the Dropbox flyer. "They put the whole thing onto Mrs. Ventrella and Deputy Packard to deal with."

"That sounds reasonable," Shay said. "Nobody else will know the identity of the suspects."

"But we need something done *now* before the show is ruined."

"Ms. Larkin will do something, don't you think?" Shay asked.

"Yes, but I don't know when she's coming back."

"Then what we are doing is the most we can do," Tessa added, seeming to come out of herself. "And we don't know if the culprits are actually in the cast. I'm sure it would make things worse if we're looking at everyone as a potential suspect."

I hated it when Tessa was reasonable.

"I just want this show to be awesome."

If I couldn't play a lead role in the production, I could play a lead role as the stage manager and prove myself at least a little. But a tiny leak could sink a big ship. And this flyer that outed the girls was far more than a tiny leak.

For the rest of the day, I considered my options. I could directly address the list—and get in trouble. I could try to find the guys who did it—but that would distract me from my most important job at the moment, and I might not figure it out anyway. *Peter Pan* had a big cast, and Northside High was a big school.

And then I had an idea. In a way, as stage manager, I was like a coach. And what does a coach do when something threatens their team? They give a pep talk.

Chapter
15

After school, I asked Shay to help me get the audio equipment from the drama room to the stage. Shay went into the closet to get the first box, and I went to the shoe organizer to grab my phone that I left during Drama 2, when Jenna walked in.

"There you are. Finally." Jenna's lips were pinched, and her normally perfect makeup looked dull.

"Yep. I had to get some things," I said as I slid my phone into my cardigan pocket.

"Mrs. Rinaldi told me I had to tell you that I'm not staying for rehearsal today." She turned to leave.

"Jenna?"

She turned back, and underneath the anger I could see that she was holding back tears.

"Is this because of the list?"

She scowled. "No!"

"I'm so sorry that happened. It's so wrong. And unfair."

She let go of the breath she was holding, and several tears slipped down her cheeks. She swore and wiped at her face.

"Can I do anything to help?"

"Why do you always act like we're friends? We're not friends." She narrowed her eyes at me.

"I know. But we're on the same team." I decided to switch tactics. "What those guys did was wrong. You have so much going for you. You're an amazing actress and singer, and you have such an important role to play. It doesn't matter what some stupid guys think. They'll end up working at McDonald's while you go on to be awesome. Don't let anyone tell you that you don't have value, because you do."

Jenna looked at me. I couldn't quite read the emotions that passed across her face. After a long moment, she nodded ever so slightly and left.

Shay shuffled over, eyes wide, her arms wrapped around a big box of audio equipment. "Whoa."

"I know." I felt bad for Jenna. Who was helping these girls through what happened? No one, as far as we knew.

"Well, that was really cool that you got to tell her that," Shay said.

"Not sure if it helped." I shrugged.

"All we can do is plant seeds. We can't make them grow."

Before rehearsal began, everyone was milling around and talking while I was plugging in the PA equipment. Mrs. Ventrella walked in and whispered something to Mrs. Rinaldi, who was sitting at the piano to the right of the stage. When she beckoned me over, I walked down the stairs and over to the piano.

Mrs. Ventrella quietly said, "Shawn Edwards will no longer be part of the cast."

I sucked in a breath. "Because of . . ."

Mrs. Ventrella lifted her eyebrows and said, "We aren't going to discuss the reasons with anyone, and you are to say nothing to the cast. We will let Ms. Larkin decide what to do when she returns."

"He has an important part—he's Mr. Darling."

"We can have someone stand in for him until a replacement has been chosen. Amelia, you can pick someone for today," Mrs. Rinaldi said.

"Okay." I walked back to the stage, scanning the cast. My eyes landed on Chad. Chad was a genuinely nice guy, dedicated, eager, and he always did a great job in class. I wasn't sure of his vocals, but it didn't matter if he was only standing in. I went over and asked him if he could be Mr. Darling for rehearsal. He didn't ask why, but instead he grinned and said, "Sure!" And Soon Li was as delighted to read Wendy's part.

It was time to start rehearsal. Per usual, everyone was spread around in various groups paying attention to no one but themselves. I turned on the portable PA. "Testing," I said into the mic. Nothing. I fiddled with the knobs. Said it again. Nothing. Unplugged the mic cord and jammed it back in. Still nothing. The thing was dead. No wonder it was stashed in the back of the closet gathering dust. I'd have to use my big-girl voice. And so much for the pep talk.

In as much excitement as I could muster, I called out a perky, "Cast!" No response. I might as well have been invisible. "ATTENTION, CAST!" A few kids looked my way but then went back to talking. Tessa and Izzy were the only ones paying attention.

In those moments when no one listened, when the hurt in my heart made a surprise appearance, I realized I really wanted people to like me. All. The. Time. I wanted to be known. I wanted to be admired. And lately, what had been most important to me was the longing to be lumped in with the "musical theater kids."

Then came a more pressing realization. In order to get people to listen, I was going to have to take charge. Enforce rules. Nobody likes the person who does that. A teacher doing that is one thing. A student doing it was something else.

I tried again. "Hey, everyone!" I called out. A couple of kids stopped talking and turned to me, but most didn't. Izzy gave me two thumbs-up signs. "PEOPLE!" I said in my best stage voice. A few more kids turned my way.

I took a deep breath, stuck two fingers in my mouth, and whistled far too loud for an indoor space. Even one as big as our auditorium.

It worked.

It was an obnoxious way to get their attention, but I couldn't argue with the effectiveness.

"Ms. Larkin is coming back Wednesday, and she's given us a list of things to practice. She asked us to be ready to finish blocking Act 2 so we can start on the Act 2 dance numbers. We're going to have to work fast though, so please, even if you're not onstage, stay in the auditorium.

"We're going to try to get through Act 1 today. Let's start with 'I Won't Grow Up.'"

I couldn't give them my full pep talk, but I could say a tiny bit. I had about fifteen seconds before I'd lose their attention. "Let's be supportive of one another. Make this a *team* effort and put out the best show this school has ever seen! Who's with me?"

The response was tepid, and I saw plenty of smirking. Eye-rolling. Oh well. If we could at least get through practice, that would be something.

During rehearsal there was a lot of whispering and chatter. Of course, people noticed Jenna and Shawn being absent. The other girls on the list were there looking a bit distracted and weary around the edges, but I hoped Operation Encouragement would be enough to keep them afloat. I watched each of them in turn, ready to give whatever support I could if I saw any signs of struggle.

And I only needed to keep the leak plugged in this boat until Ms. Larkin returned. She would keep the ship from sinking.

But during the tarantella, I heard Dev and Hayden whispering, and Shawn's name came up. When I heard it, I whirled around and said, "Pay attention to the dance."

Dev played Smee, Captain Hook's right-hand man. It was a comic part, and Dev was pretty good at playing up the funny things Smee said during the show. But real Dev was a jerk. He and Hayden were inseparable, generally crass and obnoxious.

Dev looked me up and down and snorted. "You don't count."

Hayden laughed.

I ignored the comment and pressed forward, my anger overriding everything else. "Did you two have anything to do with that list?" I hissed.

Dev smirked. "What list are you talking about?"

"There's a list?" Hayden added, feigning confusion. "Are you on the list?"

"She would never be on any list," Dev laughed.

Priya clapped her hands. "Smee, I need you over here."

Dev sauntered past, throwing me a smug look. Hayden turned to another pirate named Marcus and fake-punched him. Miranda, the other girl pirate, said, "Ignore them. They never stop."

Ignore them? My suspicions wouldn't let me. The more I watched them, the more I was certain they were behind the flyer.

When we wrapped up, I noticed Brie off by herself. I still needed to keep my promise "to support her," though I didn't understand why I had to help someone in a part she had no desire to do. I decided to try only because Ms. Larkin would ask me about it.

"Hey, Brie."

"Hey," she said.

"Is there anything I can help you with?" I asked. I had no idea what else to say.

"Why would I need help from you?" She sounded baffled.

"You tell me. Ms. Larkin asked me to help you." I should have regretted how snarky my words sounded, but after Dev and Hayden and the general negative vibe hovering over the cast, I was not in the mood to play nice.

Brie looked startled, followed instantly by a dark look. "I'm none of your business," she said and stormed off. Tessa and Izzy were scooching down a row toward me.

"Is she okay?" Tessa asked.

"I don't know," I said, the anger and frustration bubbling over. "She gets the best part in the show, and Ms. Larkin said she had to talk her into keeping it! Who does that?"

Izzy's eyes went wide. "Shhh. Amelia." Izzy glanced at the kids still hanging around, and I realized how loud my voice had gotten.

Tessa grimaced. "Probably not something you should say. Especially here."

I frowned. I refused to be scolded. "Well. It's true," I said without lowering my voice.

Tessa put her hand on my shoulder and whispered, "That's probably not something she wants anyone knowing."

I stepped back so that Tessa's hand dropped from my shoulder. "I've gotta go." I spun around and took off. I made a hard right past the curtain and ran into Wilson.

"There you are. Did you get my text?" he said.

"Oh, I . . . uh." I patted my bomber jacket and my back pockets but no phone. "I don't know where my phone is. Kind of happens to me a lot. What, um, what did you need?" I felt like a girl topside on a pitching and rolling pirate ship for the first time—tottering and trying to find her balance. I'm furious and frustrated about Brie's lack of enthusiasm for playing Peter, mad at my friends for scolding me, and then dropped into the confusing, potentially exciting world of Wilson where I'm supposed to be upbeat and eager to work on the show.

"I was hoping you'd have time to talk about the kind of lighting you want on that mountain of yours." He smiled, hands in his pockets.

"Oh . . . okay," I said and walked back onstage with him. A quick glance to the audience showed Tessa and Izzy had gone.

A small bit of relief helped me turn my attention to Wilson's request, and my rolling pirate ship found calmer waters, the deck more steady beneath me.

Although the mountain had not been built, a set of long sloping stairs to nowhere had been built at the back of the platform so we could see how high the set designer had intended the mountain to be. I started up the stairs. There were no rails to hold on to. As I got to the top, I realized how high it was. For a moment I wondered if I was too big to be up there. "Can we get light up here?" I stood near the top of the stairs. Light illuminated my legs from the knees down.

Wilson stood downstage and shaded his eyes with one hand. "Go down a few steps. Yeah. There. Would that work?"

It wasn't my show, and it shouldn't be my decision. I shrugged. "I'm sure it's fine. They enter up here, but it's not a big deal if the lights start lower. I guess."

I returned to the safety of the stage along with a growing sense of . . . calm? Ease? With all the bad going on, Wilson was a spotlight of good. Still, I felt so weird around him. Like I couldn't think quite clearly. And I didn't like that. *Why couldn't I be myself?*

I was so conflicted. I was disappointed he hadn't given me any indication that he liked me beyond working together on the show. On the other hand, I wasn't sure I wanted more than a working relationship. The possibility of more might be nice though. A bright spot to focus on.

Wilson took me around the stage, pointing out areas he thought needed light adjustments. I nodded and followed him around until I couldn't make my mother wait any longer.

When I said goodbye, Wilson smiled and said, "See ya later," and was gone. No smoothie offer. *Had I missed my one and only chance?*

Chapter

16

"WHAT DID YOUR PARENTS SAY about you being the stage manager?" Tessa asked that evening over cups of coffee, tea, and hot chocolate—with three marshmallows (for Izzy)—at Grounds and Rounds.

I looked into my tea and then glanced up, sheepish.

"You haven't told them?" Izzy asked, wiping away a chocolate mustache.

I grimaced. "Um. No." I took a drink of my chai tea.

"Your mom hasn't been curious about how late you're staying at school?" Shay asked.

"No. I told her at the beginning that rehearsals would take a lot of time." I suddenly realized how much I was avoiding or covering up these days. *Why couldn't I address uncomfortable things head-on?*

"Why ever not?" Tessa said. "It's just an announcement, no?"

"Well," I said, trying to put the puzzle pieces together in a way that would help my friends understand. "It's a bit more complicated than that. First of all, they won't know what a stage manager does and what an important role it is. Even if they are interested in grasping what I do, I'm afraid it will distract them from understanding the bigger picture of my passion for musical theater. Whenever I try to talk about that, they see it as a passing phase that I'll grow out of in six months."

"I totally get it," Shay said. "I don't much like bringing up anything that might cause conflict."

We stared at her. Tessa spoke. "Um. Wouldn't calling out your fath—uh, Mason King for abusing that horse be considered 'bringing up conflict'?"

I wanted to add, "Or that girl you shoved," and I expected the other three were thinking that as well. But none of us said it.

Shay sighed heavily. "Well. That's when my anger erupted. Not calming myself before confronting him about what ticked me off. For example, look at me with my grandmother. I don't ever talk to her about anything if I don't have to. I never know what to say to her or when a topic I thought was innocent will have her turn on me and say something that hurts."

"Exactly!" I said, holding up my chai for a toast. Shay tapped her tea to mine. "I get tongue-tied and mixed up. Then I get frustrated and angry at both myself and my parents and blurt out stupid things I didn't mean to say."

"Write a letter," Tessa said matter-of-factly. "I've written plenty to my dad. Most of which I haven't sent because that would be, well, mean to dump my fury on him."

Shay shrugged. "He deserves it."

Now Tessa sighed. "Yeah, he does. But screaming at him isn't going to change anything." She turned to look at me again. "Writing the letters have helped me sort through what I really feel and what's important to talk about." She blushed and swirled her coffee. "We've actually had a couple of good conversations that have come out of it."

"What?" Izzy said, slamming her hot chocolate down so hard a little spray misted the table. "You didn't tell us."

"Well. I guess I should explain better. The conversations were in letters, not really in person. I don't know if I can have a deep conversation with him in person. I'm liable to get distracted and angry—like you, Amelia."

"I don't know what you guys are talking about," Izzy said. "My parents are pretty easy to talk to—when they're available."

Now we looked at her.

"Braggart," Shay coughed the word out.

"So that's why you told them about Zac from the beginning?" Tessa said, cocking her head.

I nearly sputtered chai out of my mouth. In the beginning, Izzy pretty much hid the details about Zac from everyone except me.

Izzy waved her hand around. "You know what I mean."

"Back to Amelia, guys. We've gotten off track," Tessa said. She tapped the table in front of me. "What could you say in a letter that expressed how you feel—"

"But says it in a way they can connect with?" Izzy butted in. "You know. Something that helps them see things from your point of view?"

"I'm getting chocolate croissants," Shay said. "Anyone in?"

"ME!" Tessa and Izzy exclaimed. I nodded, but I was a bit lost in thought about what I would say in a letter. I couldn't come up with anything. Not yet.

Tessa and Izzy let me sit with my thoughts until Shay arrived with two huge flaky chocolate croissants cut in half. "Anyone else glad we don't have to eat gluten free?" she asked as she put the plates in the middle of the table.

"No kidding," Izzy said, not hesitating to dive into one.

"I've been doing research," I said. "Googling stuff on the internet. I suppose I could compile some of that into a letter."

"Googling what?" Izzy asked, covering her mouth full of pastry.

"Like how much it costs for kids to be involved in sports. My parents were happy to pay for Maggie's cheer and gymnastics."

"That's not cheap, is it?" Shay asked.

"No. And Josh did travel soccer."

Tessa raised her hand. "I can vouch for how expensive it is to do travel sports."

"Right!" I said. "Exactly. So why can't they spend a little money for acting, dance, or voice lessons for me? I don't get it."

We sat there munching on croissants, thinking.

"I'd also like to do more than one show a year." I took a deep breath. "It would be so magical to be able to be in shows year-round."

"How would you do that?" Shay asked.

"Well, there are only two other theaters in town that do kid-friendly musicals—"

"Great!" Izzy jumped in. "Then what's the problem? Can't you learn from doing? You know, be in as many shows as you can?"

"The problem is, they cost money. And there's a parental volunteer commitment. My parents nixed that. They're doing as much already."

The table grew quiet again.

"I texted my brother that I was trying to get Mom and Dad to see that paying for theater was no different than paying for sports. He responded with 'It costs money to do theater?'"

Shay groaned. "If your brother doesn't understand that, will your parents?"

Izzy, who had been slumping in her chair, scrolling through her phone, suddenly shot bolt upright. "Amelia, how much of the Aspire website did you get through?"

I shrugged. "Not far. Once I saw how much it cost and the parental volunteer requirement, I went to bed."

"Look," she said, tapping wildly at her screen and then waving it about so furiously that no one could see anything but a blur.

Tessa grabbed her wrist. "Okay, slow that thing down and tell us."

"Aspire has a summer camp!" she crowed. "Two weeks. This summer they're doing *High School Musical*."

A shiver ran down my spine. "Let me see." I reached for her wrist and turned her phone toward me. Another shiver. "This is totally doable. I mean, there's a fee, but it's far less than their other productions."

"And there's no volunteer requirement!" Izzy waved her phone and did a little victory dance in her chair.

I went home determined to write a straightforward letter to my parents. I had a bunch of ideas until I actually opened my laptop, and then they all vanished. So I did what any normal person would do—I cruised the internet. I started with the Aspire website, so I could get familiar with the summer camp costs and timing. Looking at the announced shows for their next season—*The Little Mermaid*, *Matilda*, and *Annie*—made my heart sigh with longing.

Baby steps, I reminded myself, and then I laughed remembering *What About Bob?*—one of Dad's favorite comedies. "Baby steps," Bob says over and over to get himself through the day.

At the bottom of Aspire's home page was a link to "blogs about the arts." I clicked on one titled, "The Arts and the Church: Why Christians should have a place in the arts."

I was astounded. The blog talked about my exact concern. From there I found several more articles that made a compelling case for Christians to be involved in the arts. I copied the links and the link to Aspire's mission statement and summer camp.

I started my letter. Stopped. Deleted. Started again. Went to Insta and Snapchat. A post from Presley popped up about her helping with the *Peter* choreography and how much fun she was having.

Presley. I pulled up her number and hesitated. *Would she respond to a text? It didn't hurt to try, to ask her questions about her theater involvement, could it?*

Me: Hey Presley! It's Amelia! It's so amazing you've already worked for Toby's Dinner Theater.
Presley: thanks

She responded!

Me: I had a question. How did you get started? 🎭😃

It took a while, but eventually she texted.

Presley: started dance at 3 😄

This was good! Easier than talking in person.

Me: Do you take acting? Or Voice?
Presley: voice, yes and I have an audition coach. 😊 mom started taking me to auditions when I was a kid. I've always done it
Me: Doing anything now?
Presley: usually do stuff at Toby's Dinner Theater. After Peter will go back. I hope.

I pulled up Toby's Dinner Theater site and found an audition page with a friendly message that there were no current auditions but to keep checking.

Me: So anyone can audition?
Presley: yep
Me: it doesn't cost anything to be in a show?
Presley: no. They pay me. But I probably was only cast because of dancing. They are always desperate for dancers.

That was a good point, and likely true. But still. Just the possibility there might be another option made my hope grow bigger than before.

After our text exchange, the email letter to my parents came pretty quickly.

Dear Mom and Dad,

I am writing you in an attempt to explain how I'm feeling. I know I'm the weird one in the family. I've always been the one who didn't like the normal things kids do. I was the one who preferred to shop at thrift stores instead of the mall. I'm okay with being the weird one. And because of that, I know sometimes you don't know what to do with me. I'm not crazy about that part, but I understand it at least.

I know theater can be expensive and time-consuming. I am willing to help in any way I can. I remember Josh and Maggie worked in the summers to help pay for the sports they chose to do. I am ready to do that too. I'll do anything to be able to do more theater. While Peter Pan *has been a challenge, it's solidified my love of musical theater.*

School only does one major production a year. If I can get involved with other theaters, I could do more. I feel like I'm already behind, and I have so much catching up to do if I'm going to study musical theater in college.

There are so many things that interest me. Like taking voice and dance lessons, being in lots more shows. But I'd like you to consider letting me start with the Aspire summer camp. There's no parent commitment, but there is a cost. Again, I'll do whatever you'd like me to do to help pay for it.

I'm including some links below to Aspire and some articles that I would like to respectfully request you read. They explain my heart so much better than I could. Once you've had a chance to read them, it would be nice to sit down together and talk about it.

I know that all of this is outside the box for our family. But I hope you will be able to see that even though it's outside the norm, it's not outside of God's heart.

Respectfully yours,
Amelia

Chapter
17

Tuesday unexpectedly brought Ms. Larkin, and even though bitterness lingered about her role in me not getting Peter, I actually sighed in relief when I saw her in Drama 1. Her presence instantly lifted a weight off my shoulders.

She sat at her desk working on her computer. When I got to her, I noticed her clothes were different. She normally wore long skirts and pretty blouses with earrings and her hair done up. But she was in plain black pants with a plain sweater, and her hair was up in a ponytail. She still looked nice. Just . . . off. Not herself.

"I have so much to talk to you about," I said.

Ms. Larkin nodded. She didn't look at me but continued typing. She was pale, too. Something was definitely wrong. "I'm sure I've already heard some of it," she said.

"You all right?" I asked. I secretly prayed that everything was fine—for utterly selfish reasons.

She looked up. "Join the class. I'm going to tell everyone at once." She moved to the whiteboard and started writing down things like "sets" and "fundraiser" and "tech" on the board.

Tell everyone what? The weight that had lifted off me came back and settled around my shoulders. I had a bad feeling.

I went and sat with Izzy, Tessa, and Shay.

"Why does your face look weird?" Shay asked.

I gestured toward Ms. Larkin. "Something's going on."

I had this sudden fear she was going to cancel the whole show. No matter how difficult it had been, I didn't want that to happen!

Ms. Larkin turned to the class, hands clasped in front of her. With her plain outfit and ponytail, she looked much younger. It was weird seeing her like that.

"Good morning, class," she said. "It's good to see you. Yes, I'm back. But only for today and half of tomorrow. Then I will be gone for an undetermined amount of time."

The class reacted with displeasure and confusion.

I leaned back on the couch, feeling sick to my stomach.

"My mother is gravely ill, and I need to go home to help care for her. She lives too far away for me to travel back and forth." She began to pace as she often did when explaining things to us. "But! The show will go on! A show like this takes a team of hardworking people, and I am confident that everyone will rise to the challenge and pull together to create an amazing show for our audiences."

I looked around. Everyone seemed sad and worried, and I felt those things too. But I also felt the crushing burden of an enormous and overwhelming project.

"First, I would like everyone to be diligent with your fundraisers and advertising. Mrs. Copeland is your point of contact for any fundraising issues and money deposits. She will be working with a flying company once we have reached our financial goal. Trust me. Peter Pan flying will be magical, so let's double our efforts.

"Second, I remind you that Mrs. Lewey will be in charge of set

decoration. Everyone is expected to help with set creating, painting, or construction—whatever needs to happen. You don't have
to be artistic or have any skill level to participate. If you're not
rehearsing or working on choreography, then you're painting or
creating. Got it?"

Murmurs of agreement swept through the room. I wondered
if anyone else was thinking what I was thinking. The set was . . .
rough. Mr. Van Hulzen had help putting the skeleton together,
but it was still mostly boards nailed into odd sculptures on rolling platforms. It took a lot of imagination to know what each
"sculpture" was supposed to be. I hoped someone else had the
imagination I lacked.

"I have a dear friend who has agreed to come in and take over
the directing of the show. You'll meet him this afternoon. I'm very
glad you'll get the chance to work with him—" She stopped for
a second, and it looked like she was trying to compose herself.
"You'll be in excellent hands. Okay. Get busy."

Izzy, Shay, Tessa, and I stared at one another in shock.

"How awful," Tessa said. Her usually straight shoulders slumped.

"I wonder what's wrong with her mom?" Izzy asked.

"Sounds bad, whatever it is," Shay added.

"I'm going to go ask her a question. I'll be right back," I said.

Ms. Larkin was talking to a couple of other girls, so I waited
nearby until she finished.

"Amelia."

"I am so sorry," I said. "I really don't know what to say."

She nodded. "It's not what I would have chosen for my life at
this moment, but it's what I need—and want—to do." She paused.
"I don't say this much in school, but I'm a woman of faith. I know
that God's will and my will are not always the same, and when
those are different, choosing His will is always best. He's a lot wiser
than me."

We kind of knew Ms. Larkin was a Christian, but she had

never been forward about it, so it seemed strange that she would talk about it now. She cocked her head and waited, but I really didn't know which issue to pull out of the tangled ones inside me.

"What's your worry?" she asked.

That was precisely the way to put it. "What am I expected to do?" I asked. I felt selfish asking, but I had to know before she left.

"I need you to continue your current role and to help the new director. You'll be able to answer questions about the blocking and the decisions we've made so far. You'll be able to help him by taking notes and keeping things organized like you did for me."

"Okay. I can do that," I said. Especially if I didn't have to run rehearsals.

"Good," she said and put her hand on my shoulder. "I would also like to ask you to keep an eye on the set decorations. There are a lot of workers, but without someone organized, like you, to make sure it's getting done, I'm afraid things might fall through the cracks. Mrs. Lewey is very sweet, but she can be, well, a bit disorganized. Make sure people are working!"

Ha! Like that would be easy. I'd already come up against everyone sitting around, talking, and playing with their phones during rehearsals. *How was I going to make them work on sets, too?*

"You'll do great," she said sincerely.

"Thank you," I said, but paused, pushing those concerns aside to address the other big issue.

"I can see there's something else on your mind."

"There is," I said and chewed on my lip for a brief moment. "What about the whole Dropbox thing?" I asked, purposely keeping my voice down. "Without a resolution, the rehearsals are very tense. Personally, I think Dev and Hayden are behind the list somehow."

Ms. Larkin sighed. "I've been briefed about the situation, and unfortunately, there's only speculation about their involvement."

I frowned. "They should be punished, though."

"Do you have one hundred percent proof they are involved?"

"No, but—"

Ms. Larkin put her hands on both my shoulders. "Let me remind you. We do not punish people on speculation of wrongdoing."

"It's horrible what someone is getting away with."

"I agree. But, Amelia, it's a very important life lesson to learn— things don't always work out the way we'd like. It's better to focus on what we *can* do rather than what we *can't* control. Make this a great show. That *can* be done, and you can play a big role in that. Don't let a few bad pirates sink the ship."

Overcome evil with good, as Izzy had said. I supposed it really was the only strategy that I could actually do something about. "Would it be all right if I organized something to make us feel more like a family?"

"What did you have in mind?"

"I was thinking about creating a 'Wall of Fame.'" I used jazz hands to emphasize. "I thought about covering the back hallway with bulletin board paper and encouraging everyone to write notes about their amazing cast members."

Ms. Larkin thought a moment. "It would need to be policed. Make sure that the notes are encouraging."

"Of course!" I said.

"And make sure no one is left out."

"My friends and I would make sure of that, I promise."

"Then go for it." She smiled sadly. "I'm sorry I won't be able to see it."

Chad walked up and said, "You asked to see me?"

Ms. Larkin gave him a nod and put her hand on my shoulder again. "You'll do great. I promise."

"Thanks," I whispered.

"Do you think she's going to be okay?" Tessa asked when I returned to the couch.

I froze, feeling awful. I wondered what was wrong with me that I hadn't even considered how Ms. Larkin was feeling. I was only worried about how the situation would affect me.

"It must be so much on her," Shay said.

"Yeah. Did you see her choke up?" Izzy asked.

They nodded somberly, and I felt like a pile of poo when, thankfully, Tessa changed the subject. "We were talking about our Thursday-night-cupcake-baking extravaganza. You in?"

"Absolutely." I didn't want to miss out again.

—◇—

Ms. Larkin repeated her little speech in Drama 2 but included a bigger push about how much work there was to do and how everyone would be needed.

I looked over the master list of committees Ms. Larkin had emailed me. She had assigned each student to a committee for costumes, sets, or props. There was a pretty good-sized list of props to gather or make for the show, and the costumes were extensive, so I was glad both those things would be someone else's responsibility.

Shay was on the tech team, and both Izzy and Tessa ended up on costumes. I wasn't thrilled to see that Jenna, Brie, and Presley were on sets with me—specifically tasked with making the mountain. I guessed I needed to take the initiative to coordinate with them.

But Jenna still wasn't at school, which worried me. Presley was working with Priya on a tricky part of her choreography. That left Brie.

Brie had her script open in her lap and was looking down at it, mumbling her lines, closing her eyes, and then saying them again. At least she was making an effort. I hoped she was getting somewhere since, starting with today's rehearsal, she wouldn't be allowed to bring the script onstage.

"How are the lines coming, Brie?" I asked, dropping to sit in front of her.

"What do you care?" she snarled without looking up.

I took a deep breath. "I'm trying to help."

"By telling everyone about a private conversation?"

I felt a sinking in my chest. Izzy and Tessa would have never repeated what I said, so if Brie knew about it, then someone else had heard and passed it along.

"Thanks to you, I have people telling me I should drop out." She hunched over her script and refused to look at me.

"I'm sor—"

Brie put up her palm. "Don't . . ." Her voice cracked. She clutched her script, leapt up, and walked away.

I should have called out to her. Or followed her. But if she didn't let me apologize, what else could I do?

When I got to rehearsal that afternoon, Ms. Larkin stood onstage talking to a young black man who had the build of a strong dancer. He had a shaved head and was wearing a black T-shirt and well-worn gray Ponto performance pants—perfect for rehearsing musicals. He was nothing like what I expected. I couldn't see the two of them hanging out in the same coffee shop, much less being close friends.

"Everyone!" Ms. Larkin called out. "I'd like you to meet the incomparable Kenny Solomon."

He smiled and gave a stage bow.

"I've known Mr. Solomon for a long time. He comes to us with years of NYC-level experience. We are very lucky to have him with us, and I know you'll learn so much."

Kenny put his hand on his chest with a "who, me?" expression.

"He'll be watching our rehearsal today, so he can see where we are." She clapped twice. "Let's get going. Amelia?" She pointed at me, and I met them at the bottom of the stairs.

"Can you sit next to Mr. Solomon and answer any questions he might have?"

"You have to stop calling me Mr. Solomon, Risa. All wrong. So wrong. Can't they call me Kenny?"

"It's up to you," Ms. Larkin said.

"Then it's Kenny!" His arm shot up as he pointed toward the ceiling.

I laughed.

Ms. Larkin called for everyone to start at the beginning and get as far as possible into the show.

Kenny turned to me. "Amelia, huh? That's like an old lady name."

I laughed. "I guess."

"You named after a grandma or something?" he asked as we both took seats in the first row.

"Nope."

Kenny shrugged and leaned forward. "So are these losers any good?"

I opened the thick notebook in my lap and glanced his way. "You're not a teacher, are you?" I asked.

"Why do you say that? I teach."

"Teachers don't usually call us losers," I said.

"Oh, it's a term of endearment, trust me. So what about you? What's your story? Why are you down here with the notebook and not up there?"

"I'm just a pirate," I said.

"Interesting."

"What does that mean?"

Kenny had that vibe that made me feel I could talk to him like a normal person rather than a teacher. He shrugged with one shoulder, then looked at me, as if he was assessing me. "I get it. You got that character look happening."

"Meaning . . . ?"

Kenny turned his attention to the stage and watched the scene unfold. He pointed to Soon Li, who was reading Jenna's part. "Who's Wendy? She's good."

"Soon Li. She's standing in for our Wendy." Jenna still hadn't appeared, and Ms. Larkin hadn't said anything about her whereabouts.

"Oof. Peter need to learn her lines," Kenny commented.

That was the truth. Brie's script was gone, and she was asking for every single line.

"Risa told me you're supposed to help her out?"

"Yeah," I said. "She's not thrilled with that idea."

"Girl needs serious help."

As the rehearsal progressed, Kenny kept a running commentary. "I like the choreography." "She's pretty good. I see some sparks." "That kid's got potential."

I had never met anyone like him. He seemed so bold and fearless, and I kind of liked him.

When we got to the pirate scenes, I stayed put. Nobody would notice.

"Wait, aren't you a pirate?" Kenny asked.

"It's fine. I'm just in the back," I said.

Kenny shot me a look, but I couldn't tell what it meant.

"Tell me about New York City," I said when he didn't say any more.

"New York City. The city that will raise you up and tear you apart. Sometimes in one afternoon."

"Oh, I wanna go there so bad. Is it wonderful?"

"Yeah, wonderful. Terrible. Tragic. Amazing."

"Are you an actor?" I asked. "Like, do you do this for a living?"

"Yeah, but it ain't no living. It's one job to the next. I mean, look at me. Sitting in a high school auditorium? Risa lucky she caught me in a homeless moment." Kenny laughed.

"What have you been in?" I asked.

Kenny screwed up his face. "Nah, girl. You need to get them stars out of your eyes and get a real education." He laughed again, joking, but not joking.

I planned to get an education from this NYC pro—even if all I could do was watch and learn.

Chapter
18

THE FIRST THING I did after rehearsal was look up Kenny online. Before Mom pulled up, I found his résumé and a handful of other sites where his name appeared on the cast list. He had a lot of credits. Nothing huge like Broadway, but he had performed in or choreographed more than twenty shows. He was living the life.

"Why'd you send us an email?" Mom asked before I even put on my seat belt.

"I thought writing down my thoughts would help me think them through."

"Makes sense. Let's talk after dinner?" Her expression was all business, but I could live with that.

"Yeah, that sounds good!" I was excited despite her cautious tone. It was fine. I would convince them. Aspire had a summer camp, and other people out in internet land agreed with me that the arts were important!

When we got home, I did my homework at the kitchen table, which I had rarely done since elementary school, simply so I could be present. I tried to ask her a few questions while she finished up dinner, but she told me to wait.

The pit in my stomach grew throughout dinner as Mom and Dad chatted about church stuff (always), Josh stuff (sometimes), and Maggie stuff (not often because she was Miss Perfect). It wasn't until the dinner dishes were neatly loaded in the dishwasher, the entire gray-and-white Joanna Gaines kitchen was spotless, and our shiplap dining room table was wiped down that Mom finally said, "Ready?"

I slipped into my chair, feeling like I was in trouble. I reminded myself that I had asked for the meeting. I folded my hands so I wouldn't fidget. Fidgeting annoyed Mom.

Dad took off his glasses and leaned back in the chair. "How's *Peter Pan* going?"

I tried to smile, but it stuck there awkwardly on my face in the fake in-between. I settled for a one-shoulder shrug and said, "Fine." There seemed to be too much to explain.

Dad frowned. "We're going to need more than that. You said you were going to quit. You stayed. But we haven't really talked about it since."

"It's really busy. The usual theatrical intensity," I said. I seriously had hoped to focus on the "next," not the "now."

Mom leaned back and folded her arms. I could see the backyard behind her. It was perfectly landscaped. In a few weeks it would be green, and a collection of chairs would be taken from storage and placed on the stone patio around the firepit. My mother's decorating gene had missed me completely.

She was perfect too. She wore dress pants and a green blouse topped with a pale blue cardigan. So simple. She always looked elegant somehow. I'd missed that gene too. I was wearing a thrift shop skirt with a T-shirt and a sloppy mustard-colored cardigan.

CHASING THE SPOTLIGHT || 151

"In the beginning *Peter Pan* was important to you," Mom said. "So we'd like to hear more about it." Her tone was even. Patient. "You really don't share much with us."

I decided, like Tessa, it would be better if I did all communication through email so I could be careful about what I said, rather than let words randomly fly out of my mouth.

"Can't we talk about what comes next?" I asked.

"We will," Dad said. They exchanged glances. I swear they had whole conversations with their eyes. I had no clue what they were "saying," but something about it made me very nervous.

They sat there. Waiting. Giving nothing away. I knew their endurance level was far greater than mine. Okay. I would tell them the basics. Keep emotions out of it. A tricky situation because although I felt good about being stage manager, I still felt sick about being a pirate. I didn't expect them to understand. They would only see that I will have plenty of chances to perform in other shows, not why losing the Peter role hurt so much nor why it was so important. I ran my fingers through my short hair. I wondered what they would say if I told them how hard I had prayed for that role.

"Well, Ms. Larkin asked me to be the stage manager. Which is really cool because it's an important job."

"Really? Tell us more about that," Dad said.

I went through some of the things I had already done like creating spreadsheets and contact lists. I showed them the fundraising Instagram feed. Explained my other responsibilities, including keeping track of the location of everyone and everything onstage, plus the work committees, and filled them in on Ms. Larkin leaving and how that impacted my role as stage manager. I left out the Dropbox mess, Brie, and Wilson.

"That sounds very positive," Mom said.

I nodded.

"Impressive. Sounds like a lot of responsibility," Dad added. "I'm sure you'll learn a lot too."

"Oh yeah, a ton. One thing I'm learning is that musicals are what I really want to do in the future. But the high school does only one musical a year—it's not their main focus. That's why it's important I go to Aspire. So I can train more." I looked at each of them. "I'm hoping you see that I'm doing what you asked me to do. Putting my best into this show."

"We're glad to hear that," Dad said.

"Amelia. You know that you have always been a bit headstrong and impulsive." Mom looked at me like she didn't mean it in a totally bad way. "The theater idea took us a little by surprise since you showed no interest before you started high school."

"You're saying this 'theater thing' will be your focus for the rest of your life, but this is still pretty new to us," Dad said. "Judging by the articles you sent, it seems you are under the impression we are against the arts in general—we're not. We think it's wise to take it one step at a time. For all of our sakes."

I twisted a stray thread from my cardigan around my finger over and over again, biting back my disappointment. *One step at a time. That was better than a flat-out no, wasn't it?* I had unrealistically hoped I could get them to agree that I could participate in every show possible for the next two years. Since they wouldn't, there was no point in pushing for extra musicals. I had to slow down and be okay with resigning myself to the "one step at a time" path. "Could I start with theater summer camp? It's only two weeks, and there's no parent commitment."

My parents had a silent conversation, and then Dad said, "Let your mom and me talk about it and pray, okay?"

I nodded.

Praying about it? The idea made me feel sad. *What if God said no to that, too?*

Chapter
19

THURSDAY AT LUNCH I sat with Tessa, Shay, and Izzy as they talked through their cupcake-making plans for the evening.

At some point, they noticed that I looked grumpy.

"You okay?" Izzy asked. She took a big bite of her cheeseburger, squirting mustard all over Tessa's salad.

"Izzy!" Tessa moved it away while Izzy snort-laughed and tried to swallow her burger.

"Sorry," Izzy said, sounding like her mouth was full of cotton.

Shay rolled her eyes at them and then said to me, "What's wrong?"

What was wrong? My parents hadn't given me a solid answer about Aspire, I was overwhelmed with the Peter stuff, and Ms. Larkin had pulled me aside before she left to remind me that she really believed in Brie and wanted me to help her reach her "potential." Why was that my job? "Probably PMS," I lied. "How's Operation Encouragement going?"

We all looked at Izzy. "Good, I think." She twirled a curl around her finger. "I can't stop thinking about how awful it must be for the other girls. I'm guessing that like me, they probably hoped the pictures would all go away or stay secret forever. Then someone exposes your shame for everyone to see." She shuddered and looked away.

Ms. Larkin had given the cast a very firm lecture that the Dropbox topic was off-limits and that anyone harassing a cast member would be at risk of being removed. I hoped it would shut Dev and Hayden up, but the damage had already been done.

"Is there anything being done to take care of them?" Tessa asked.

"I asked Mrs. Ventrella about that," I said. "The girls were all encouraged to go see one of the guidance counselors if they wanted to talk."

"That's all they told me, too," Izzy said.

"That doesn't seem like enough," Tessa said.

"Our encouragement is a good thing," Shay said. "But is there anything else we can do to help these girls?"

Lunch chatter surrounded us as we chewed in silence.

"I haven't had any response from Jenna, and she still hasn't come to school," I finally said. "I'm worried about her."

"Invite her to make cupcakes with us tonight!" Izzy said.

I laughed.

"Can't hurt to ask," Tessa said. "Reaching out matters even if she says no."

It was as good a reason as any.

> Me: We'd like you to come make cupcakes with us tonight.
> Jenna: We? Us?
> Me: Izzy Shay Tessa

A long wait.

Jenna: I can't

"She can't," I told the girls. "But it was a good idea. If the school isn't going to do more for the girls on the list, what if we invited them to get together in a safe space to talk? See how they're doing."

"I wonder if Zoe would come. She'd know how to help," Tessa suggested. Zoe was one of the youth group leaders at Tessa and Izzy's church.

"Oh my stars, that would be perfect," Izzy said.

The plan was formed quickly with the bookstore after hours as a safe location. We had to wait to hear from Shay's aunt and Zoe so we could confirm a time.

I looked down at my conversation with Jenna.

Me: I'm here if you want to talk ☺

It was a long wait but eventually:

Jenna: thanks

The sub in Drama 2 handed me a note from Kenny. I showed it to her, and she agreed to let me fulfill Kenny's request in the auditorium.

I sat in the center of the auditorium as Kenny had asked. He wanted me to get a head start on my role of seeing how the sets should be placed onstage when they were being used and how to arrange them backstage when they weren't needed. It was a puzzle to keep the sets in order and placed where they could quickly be found and put into position by the tech people.

I had my white notebook in my lap, mechanical pencil, and preprinted stage layout. I liked this kind of challenge. Finding ways to be organized and efficient. And I was kind of proud of

myself that Kenny thought I could do this. I decided to look at the
entire stage from the perspective of the audience first and imagine
the best position for the sets. Then I would go check out backstage
with set layout and storage in mind.

I should have turned on the stage lights before I sat down. I
sighed and felt too lazy to get up and go all the way down to hit
the switches.

I stared at the ghost light softly illuminating the stage. The
odd sculptures of yellowish-white wood on rolling platforms were
scattered in a haphazard fashion—placed where they were most
easily worked on. The scene looked more like a bizarre skate park
than Neverland. I couldn't imagine how they could ever become
something different. Something more.

I tapped my pencil on the paper, trying to get a vision of what
should go where. But I couldn't seem to land my thoughts. I kept
being drawn to these shapes that seemed nothing like what they
would become.

I thought about my family and how they found it difficult to
have the imagination to see me as something more. I could hardly
blame them. I wasn't a neat and perfect girl, quiet and demure,
attending youth group, singing in the choir, wearing pretty little
dresses that would place me firmly in my family's neat and perfect
world of church and normalcy and traditional pursuits. I wasn't
supersmart—just an average student—and therefore not into
forensic teams or robotics or debate. Sports made me feel out of
place and awkward. I was too uncoordinated and heavy to do any
of them well.

For my whole life there didn't seem to be any place for someone like me. But then, like the best surprise gift ever, along came
drama my freshman year. It only took a couple of weeks to become
aware that I belonged here. Picked first, rather than last. A growing leader rather than a flustered, floundering follower. Soon after
that, I realized the theater world is where I could be myself and

be fully accepted. I could be weird and loud, and most everyone shrugged and thought that was normal. As an actress, exhilaration swept through me when I took on the heart and outlook and point of view of someone else. I *became* a homeless person or a mother or a grocery store clerk or a talking bear, table, or lamp.

The spring musical was a focal point from September on. Everyone went on and on about how amazing it was to be a part of the production and how you *had* to try out for it. I couldn't wait. Then tryouts came, and I choked. Failing to follow through on the audition was like failing to join the world I was destined to belong to and succeed in. Worse, it wasn't that the musical theater world had rejected *me*. I had failed to even knock on the door.

Maybe I longed for it too much. I had finally found a place to belong and could imagine myself in this world so strongly that when it came time to leap, I faltered.

When Northside's production of *Seussical* opened, I sat in the audience and was instantly captivated by Angelina Carballo playing the lead. I watched in awe, mesmerized by how sweet and funny and genuine and perfect she was in the role of Gertrude. She had the entire audience believing she was truly a bird in love with Horton, but not accepting herself. The audience accepted her. Embraced her. Applauded her.

The experience nearly overwhelmed me. Thoughts and desires surged like a tsunami—I can do that! I *want* to do that! It became my dream, my goal.

It was so all-consuming that I hadn't considered what it would be like to be one of the nameless characters onstage. Had I noticed the jungle animals or the Who ensemble last year? I sure didn't remember them. I remembered the stars. The ones who took center stage, positioned under the spotlight, commanding the attention of the vast, dark audience. I saw the ones who got roses right before the final curtain fell. The ones who, at the end of the show, had snaking lines of little kids asking for pictures and autographs.

Nobody asks for a picture with a pirate.

Being Peter would have brought the validation I longed for: You fit here! You belong here!

I put my hands over my face. *How had I ever thought Peter was within my reach? Or that a haircut was necessary to give me an edge?*

I understood now that praying for Peter had been more than just praying for a part. I was asking God if I belonged onstage like I believed. I wanted His stamp of approval. "Yes, Amelia, you belong!"

But God said no.

I didn't know what to do with that.

The articles I read made it sound like the arts were absolutely in God's heart. That God made people like Broadway stars and movie stars and famous painters and sculptors and singers just as assuredly as He made Bible teachers and plumbers and engineers. But while the articles made sense in my brain, my heart was longing for God to prove it to me.

I didn't understand.

Why wasn't God helping me?

Chapter
20

"Amelia?"

Wilson appeared in front of me.

"You okay?"

I shrugged.

"You're missing class?"

"Yeah."

"I can leave you alone if you like." He shifted. Adjusted his glasses. Moved his hair aside.

"You can stay," I said. *I want you to stay.* Truly, I needed to get out of my head and get busy. "Actually, can you help me with something?" I asked.

"Yes!"

I was taken aback by his enthusiasm, but it was nice.

I explained my plan as I led the way to Mrs. Rinaldi's office where we got what we needed: green bulletin board paper, blue paper for lettering, scissors, wall tack, and tape.

Wilson got the ladder from the stage, and he fastened the rolls up high on the hallway wall while I smoothed the paper along the wall to the floor and cut an even edge. "Have you ever auditioned for a show?" I asked.

"Nope," he laughed. "I'm a behind-the-scenes kind of guy."

"What do you get out of it? I mean, the actors get this attention and applause. What do you get?"

He furrowed his brow. "I don't understand."

"You do a ton of work for the show, but you're invisible. The set people, costumers, and techs do so much work but are never onstage and don't get any applause or recognition." I rolled some wall tack and stuck balls of it in intervals under the paper low to the ground.

He shrugged. "Well, yeah. But those things don't matter to me."

"Why not?" I genuinely wanted to understand, and he genuinely seemed confused by my question. All I knew was how it felt to experience the vastness of the stage yet be firmly set somewhere magical, living a life that was not yours in front of an enraptured audience.

"You know how the credits at the end of a movie seem to roll forever?" he asked. "Every person on that long list had a hand in making that movie. Each one is necessary to create something much bigger than themselves. And I chose to be one of those people. To fill a need and help make the bigger thing happen." He shrugged. "That's enough for me."

I looked up at his face, so open and honest. So real. I handed the last roll up to him. When he took it, there was this . . . I don't know, energy, between us that made me nervous, so I looked away.

"You're doing an awesome job as stage manager," he said.

I snorted. "Some things are going well, and others . . . I don't know how to fix." I thought about the Dropbox girls—especially Brie and Jenna, who were truly an important part of our show. Even though Jenna was being snarky to me, I had some sympathy for what she might be going through. But Brie? It was like my heart turned to stone with her.

"Shows are always messy," he said, letting the roll unfurl down the wall to me. "Being on this side of a production is like being a firefighter. Every production has fires that pop up. You get used to watching for them and then putting them out one by one."

"I've been imagining it like a leaky boat. Same thing, right?"

"Exactly."

I knelt by the blue paper and outlined large letters for "Wall of Fame."

I thought about exploring my concerns about the show with him. *Was it wise to open up to a guy I didn't know well? One I was starting to like a little?* Would being super honest scare him off? If it did, maybe that was okay. I dove in. "This show hasn't been anything like what I thought it would be." He was quietly tacking the top of the paper near the ceiling, so I continued. "I've dreamed of performing on the big stage for so long, I thought for sure I'd get a real part."

"Didn't dream of being a pirate, huh?" he asked.

I snorted. "Yeah. I was chasing Peter Pan and landed on a pirate ship."

He laughed.

"I guess that makes me sound like a jerk. But no, I didn't. And to see people who don't even want them get the best parts . . ."

"Ohhh," he said. "Yeah. I've heard a few people mention that. That stuff about Brie probably isn't true. Just another little fire."

"Yeah." I re-tucked my hair under the beanie as though trying to hide my shame. *What would Wilson think of me if he knew the truth?* I had not intentionally started a rumor. Someone had taken my little temper tantrum and ran with it. But still. There wouldn't be any talk at all if I hadn't mouthed off out of my own anger and frustration.

I cut around the letters I'd drawn on the blue paper.

"Amelia, you don't need to feel bad about being a pirate," Wilson said, coming down from the ladder. He picked up the other pair of scissors and began to cut letters out. "The pirates are important in this show."

I scoffed before I could stop myself.

"My dad's a pastor, so he's kind of in a spotlight every Sunday. He always says, 'For every hour in the pulpit, spend ten in the trenches.' He's scrubbed bathrooms, made food, washed dishes. He never expected anyone to do a job that he wouldn't do himself. His words and example stuck with me. Of course, it's probably easier for me. I have no desire to be on a stage. I kind of like being in the trenches. The trench work is vital. For the show. And us as individuals."

My thoughts swirled. I sort of understood what he was saying but didn't particularly like it.

"Aspire teaches that in its own way. They expect everyone to learn about each of the roles and pieces that go into a production. They focus on serving. They pray before starting. Other than that, Aspire isn't that different from what we do right here. The work? It's the same kind of work." He set aside the *F* he'd cut out and started cutting the *A*. "You know, it doesn't cost anything to volunteer with Aspire." He looked up at me. "Come with me Saturday. See what you think."

More volunteer work? More invisibility? *More Wilson.*

"Um," I said, hoping not to sound too eager. "Maybe."

Chapter
21

WHEN I GOT TO REHEARSAL, I spotted Jenna sitting in the auditorium off by herself and was relieved that she was there. She didn't have her normal confidence, for sure. But at least she was here. Ever since Tessa's best friend, Mackenzie, attempted suicide, the thought had lodged itself in my brain—you didn't really know what was going on behind happy smiles. I didn't know if Jenna was actually feeling depressed, but I couldn't shake being worried that she could be. And no one would know.

Kenny stood onstage, pacing in a relaxed way, sizing everyone up as they came in and dropped their backpacks on the auditorium chairs. He was wearing his gray workout pants and a black T-shirt with a faded *Hamilton* logo on it. He used one finger to beckon me over when I arrived.

"I have had three of these teenagers pull me aside and 'encourage' me to replace Peter. Do you know what's going on?"

I inwardly cringed. But before I could decide how to answer, he kept going.

"Risa insisted that Brie needed to be Peter and that you would back her up? Yes?"

"Yes." The word came out small. I didn't know how to explain what was happening unless I also explained Brie's valid reason to be furious with me.

"All right then." Kenny sighed. "Make it work."

"Okay," I said, not feeling the least bit confident. I then hurriedly described the Wall of Fame project and asked if I could explain it to the cast. He agreed. At exactly three o'clock he cleared his throat and held his arms out wide.

"I know Ri—Ms. Larkin introduced me yesterday. Again, I'm Kenny. Do not call me Mr. Solomon. I will be your fearless director to bring this baby home. As you can see, I'm kind of different from Ms. Larkin, but don't you fret! You work. I'll work. And this will work!"

A few hoots and hollers from the cast. They seemed to like his energy. He exuded it.

"All yours," Kenny said to me and stepped back.

"Ms. Larkin did a great job reminding us we need to work together to pull off a fantastic show." I purposefully looked at Dev and Hayden, but they didn't seem to be intimidated. "Every person in this show matters. We need to build each other up—*not* tear each other down." My own words seemed to scoop out a pit in my stomach. I could not look at Brie. "I'm sure some of you saw the board in the back hallway—our new 'Wall of Fame.' This wall is a place to publicly encourage your castmates. Tell them what they are doing great. Tell them what you appreciate about them. Keep it positive. Motivational. Let's give Ms. Larkin the fantastic show she deserves."

Izzy and Tessa enthusiastically started applause that spread through the cast. Dev and Hayden didn't applaud, but they didn't roll their eyes or exchange snarky looks. I would take that as a win.

But Brie. I snuck a look over at her where she was sitting cross-legged, script in lap and face in her hands.

Kenny stepped forward. "Everyone got that? Okay! Let's get Act 2 finished so we can run, run, run. We gonna move quick so keep up! Pirate ship up first! Wait." He looked around, baffled. "What are we doing for a pirate ship?"

Mrs. Lewey walked onstage wringing her hands. She was younger than most of the other teachers but always had a frazzled air about her. She pointed to a large brown pole upstage center. "We will have two giant sails attached to that mast . . ." I tuned out as she continued to explain the pirate ship to Kenny.

I perched on the edge of the stage, unsure what Kenny expected me to do here. *Was I supposed to cue? Take notes? Take my place onstage as a pirate? Be available for whatever?*

Mrs. Lewey finished, and Kenny positioned Peter and Hook for their main fight. He rounded up Lost Boys and pirates to pair them for the fight scene.

He caught my eye and scowled. "Aren't you in this scene?"

I shrugged.

He lifted an eyebrow and stared at me until I went over to him.

"Girl. Don't ever turn down a chance to be on a stage." He put his hands on my shoulders. "Every moment you get to be up here is a glorious opportunity. Don't waste it."

I felt scolded and went to stand where he pointed, near Izzy and Tessa.

"The Wall sounds a-ma-zing," Izzy gushed.

"Brilliant idea," Tessa added.

I forced a smile. Funny how mention of the Wall only made me feel worse about Brie.

"Lost Boys," Kenny called out. "Over here. Pronto. Chop-chop!" The "boys" scurried over to Kenny, who grabbed their shoulders and placed them one by one exactly where he wanted them. Then he commanded the pirates, pointing at us one at a time. "You! Over here," he said to me, finally. He positioned me in front of a skinny freshman boy named Malique. This kid was about my height, but one-third my diameter. I told myself to be careful not to use too much force during the fight. I was worried I'd throw him right offstage.

Kenny taught us the basic elements of stage fighting that we would use for this scene. "Remember, we are creating the *illusion* of fighting. Not actually punching each other—no matter how much you might like to."

A few of the boys groaned their disappointment. They had already been putting each other in headlocks and grabbing shirts or waistbands to fling each other around.

Malique never stood still. He jumped up and down and did boxer shuffles while he waited to learn the next move. "This is so fun," he said. Over and over. "Isn't this fun?"

I tried not to roll my eyes.

Once everyone had mastered the basics, Kenny gave each pair of fighters a different order of the moves we had just learned so the battle looked as real as possible. Kenny seemed happiest during this frenzied pace of the pirate ship battle. It seemed to me there was so much happening at once, I wondered what it would look like to an audience. Up close, it was barely organized chaos.

When we took a break, Izzy and Tessa came over with their water bottles.

"This is going to be such a cool scene!" Izzy said.

"Who knew you could get exercise doing theater?" Tessa said with a laugh.

Kenny yelled for everyone to run it one more time before we moved to the final nursery scene.

"We're starting at six tonight," Izzy interjected quickly. "And we talked to Zoe so we can solidify our plans for the weekend, too."

During the nursery scene I sat with the script, made notes, and fed lines to Brie the whole time. Twice Kenny pointed at me and pointed at Brie, but I had no idea what he expected me to do in the middle of rehearsal. Besides, if I were her, I wouldn't want me helping either.

Before we left, Kenny walked by and said over his shoulder, "Get those lines in her, ya hear?"

I pressed my lips together. Kenny expected me to fix her, but I honestly didn't know how. Memorizing lines seemed so easy to me, so I guessed she wasn't trying hard enough. I knew her lines. I knew most of the lines for most of the cast for Act 1. And Brie had gotten her script immediately after the cast list went up, so she had no excuse for not knowing them. *Why was this my problem to solve?*

Except it was now. It felt wildly unfair. I didn't understand why Ms. Larkin insisted on having Brie do the role even after she didn't want it. *Would replacing her be so bad?*

Brie had her backpack on and was walking up the aisle toward the back of the auditorium when I caught up with her.

"Hey, Brie," I called out to stop her.

She turned, a sour look on her face. "What?"

"Maybe we can get together and run your lines?"

"I'm fine," she said, then turned to leave again.

"Wait. I want to help. I'm really good at memorizing lines. And . . . we have to."

She scowled. "What is that supposed to mean?" She shifted her backpack and sighed like I was keeping her from something important.

"Look. Ms. Larkin and Kenny told me I have to help you, so you might as well take the help," I said.

"Why would they say that?" Instead of looking mad, she looked . . . worried, maybe.

"You don't know your lines, and you're supposed to be off book."

"We just started Act 2. I'll get them. It'll be fine," she said and walked off.

What was I supposed to do? Was I off the hook if she refused? I'd have to make it clear to Kenny that she refused my help.

I went back to the stage where I found Mrs. Lewey half under the mountain.

"Amelia? Is that you?" She extricated herself and rubbed her hands together.

"Yes, Mrs. Lewey."

She adjusted her purple-framed glasses, the lenses catching the ghost light that had already been turned on. "You girls need to start on this soon. There's a lot to do before this actually looks like a mountain." She looked around. "Where's the rest of your mountain committee? I told Ms. Larkin the mountain needed four people."

"I don't know," I said sheepishly. I'd forgotten we were supposed to meet. I had texted them yesterday that we were to meet Mrs. Lewey after rehearsal today . . . and then spaced. Now I didn't see Jenna or Presley anywhere. And Brie was already gone. "I told them, but . . ."

Mrs. Lewey waved her hand in the air. "I don't have time to wait for them. I'll show you what to do. It's not that hard. Just time-consuming." She went to the wall at the back of the stage and grabbed a giant roll of chicken wire that was every bit as tall as her. She started dragging it to the mountain platform. I jumped in to help her, but even though she was short, she didn't have any problem wrangling the thing. She unrolled a section and held up a heavy-duty snipper with a thick, green plastic handle. "Be careful with these," she said in a bright tone. "I didn't tell Mr. Lewey I was borrowing them, so don't lose them! I don't want to have to explain that I've lost yet another of his tools at a school function."

She turned away and gestured at the mountain frame. "The chicken wire is the key to the mountain. It gives us the stability to build and shape it any way we like. Attach the chicken wire with a staple gun at the top like this, then run it down to the bottom so that you cover the whole thing. Then you'll stuff anything you can find from the recycling bins underneath the wire and mold it until it takes on the shape of a real mountain. Do one section at a time. Once the mountain has its shape, we finish it with layers of papier-mâché and paint."

I nodded. I was pretty sure I understood, but the logistics of making it actually happen stressed me out a bit. This was like a giant craft project, and I wasn't a craft project kind of girl. I was nervous about Jenna, Presley, and Brie being on my committee. I hadn't said anything when I saw their names on my committee, because in the back of my mind I thought maybe it would help me get connected with them. Be seen as one of those musical theater girls. But they weren't doing anything. Their fundraising project was still not settled, and I doubted they intended to follow through on one.

"Sometimes you have to jump in feetfirst," Mrs. Lewey was saying. "It'll make more sense once you get going. I'll check in on you, and you can come by if you have questions. I have to scoot. You going to be okay?"

I nodded even though I was pretty sure the answer should be no.

She offered me the wire cutters on her outstretched flat hands as though presenting a precious gift. "Don't lose them!"

"Yes, ma'am," I said. I took them. She patted me on the shoulder, and then she was gone, leaving me with a giant roll of chicken wire and a mountain.

I wrestled with the chicken wire, certain it had a mind of its own, determined to thwart me at every effort. To keep myself from uttering words of frustration, I thought about my conversation with Wilson.

I wasn't sure I could be like him. *Could I love theater even if I wasn't ever in the spotlight?* Sounds and images of sitting in the delighted audience at *Seussical* swept by. It had been hard to sit on the sideline with minimal involvement in the show. I yearned for more. And now, although I didn't have it all, I did have plenty more than I had last year. *Could playing a smaller part onstage be better than sitting in a captivated audience?* I had to admit that what little I had this year was so much better than last. But being a pirate still felt awful inside. A reminder of God's firm *no*.

I tried to attach the wire. Mrs. Lewey had made it look so easy.

I had imagined becoming Peter would be a true adventure. Now, instead of the adventure I had anticipated, I was on the sidelines plugging leaks—and I wasn't doing a very good job of it. I had alienated two of the three girls I had hoped to impress and made Brie's difficult situation worse with my own big mouth.

I hated the resentment that swelled in me when I thought of Brie. She didn't deserve the role of Peter. I would have worked my tail off for it, and she's not even bothering to learn her lines! My stomach soured as I again considered the irony of being tasked to help her succeed in a role she doesn't even want.

Jesus. Please help me with this mess.

After forty-five minutes of wrestling with my thoughts and the chicken wire, all I had to show for it was one three-foot strip of wire, sweaty armpits, and a brain tired of endless, repetitive, simple prayers. When Mr. Mercedes, one of our nighttime janitors, stopped in a second time to lock up, I tucked the cutters in a safe place, texted Mom, and went out front to wait for her.

During dinner I set down my fork and said, "Can I go to Aspire on Saturday?"

My parents looked at each other and then me with confused expressions.

"How about we back that up and start at the beginning?" Mom said.

"The beginning of what?" I said.

"You launch into asking permission for something, and we have no details," Dad explained as he passed the potatoes to Mom.

I sighed. "Aspire has rehearsals on Saturdays, and I'd like to go check it out since . . ."

"Since what?" Mom said.

"Since I still really want to go to that camp. Have you talked about it yet?" My parents were sometimes slow to give an answer, especially if it was something that wasn't directly school related. They said yes to those pretty quickly.

Dad laughed. "Millie, you look like Felix begging for food at the table. You have a very expressive face."

Mom laughed, too, but I was too busy trying to figure out what that had to do with the camp situation.

"You can do the camp," Dad said. "We both think that's a reasonable next step. As long as you keep giving your best to your school show."

I jumped up and threw my hands in the air. "Yes!" The excitement of having a "next step" to look forward to shot a bolt of electricity through me.

"The whole theater world is a bit of a mystery to us, Mills. We need you to explain things better. How can you go to Aspire rehearsals if you're not part of it?" Dad added.

"You can volunteer. I mean, I can volunteer. They always need lots of help, and Wilson said it would be a good way to get involved and see what it's like."

"Who's Wilson?" Mom asked.

"A friend from school. He volunteers there."

"The boy you were with last week?"

"Yes. He helps out with every production at school and at lots of the other theaters."

"He's . . . just a friend?" Dad asked.

"Yes. A friend." I tried not to squirm in my seat. Although it was true we were only friends, I was also hyperaware of the little fluttery feelings I had when his name came up. I wondered if my parents could see that on my face too. "He offered to take me and introduce me to some people. He said they like having volunteers."

"Is something going on with this boy?" Mom asked. "Do you like him?"

"We're just friends." *Flutter, flutter.*

Did I like Wilson? Did I like the idea of a possibility of something more with him? Something that had literally never happened to me, ever? I made myself take a deep breath and keep my voice steady. "Wilson is a friend. He's involved with Aspire, and I'd like to check it out. Please?"

"Well, I don't know about some boy we don't know driving you," Mom said.

"That's okay. You can drop me off, and I can meet him there. Whatever works."

They agreed, which made me squeal again.

While I cleaned up after dinner, I thought about how I had assumed that God said no to my place in theater when I didn't get Peter. *So did this change mean anything?* I wasn't sure, but I wanted to cry in utter relief.

When I got to my room, I texted Wilson:

Me: I can go Saturday! I will meet you ☺
Wilson: Great! I think you'll like it ☺

Chapter
22

ALL THE WAY TO IZZY'S, I couldn't stop thinking about Wilson's winky-face text. *Did he send everyone winky faces? He didn't seem to be the winky-face type. So did the one he sent me mean anything or not?*

I arrived late to the cupcake-baking party. They were already two pans in when I got there but cheered when I popped into the kitchen. That felt good. Shay was elbow-deep in soapsuds at the sink, Tessa was nervously mixing ingredients in a giant stand mixer, and Izzy had a piping bag poised over a dozen cupcakes on a cooling rack.

"What can I do?" I asked.

"You can dry those," Shay said, pointing to a pile of upturned dishes, foamy bubbles dripping from her arm.

"Dish towels are in the bottom drawer next to the oven," Izzy said, pointing with her foot.

While I dried, the girls gave me an update on Operation Encouragement. Shay's Aunt Laura had said that we could have the bookstore to ourselves for an hour after closing on Sunday, and Zoe said she'd be happy to be there. It was perfect.

"Will they come, though? I'd be kind of intimidated," Shay said.

"It would be a scary step. But going through it alone seems worse," Tessa said. "Oh no. I lost count! Izzy!"

Izzy looked inside the mixing bowl, piping bag still in both hands. "Add half a cup."

Tessa laughed and tossed up her hands. "How can you tell?"

Izzy shrugged.

"Let's invite them right now," I said.

Izzy brushed her hair from her face with her arm, getting a bit of green frosting on her temple. "How about we invite them after we get the next batch in the oven?"

Shay rinsed a cupcake tin and propped it on top of a large bowl. "That's what I like about you, Amelia. You dive right in to get things done that are important to you."

The moment the oven door closed on the next batch, we stopped and took out our phones. I texted Jenna, Shay texted Fatima, Tessa texted Corinna, and Izzy texted Selena and Dee.

Then I took pics for the #HelpPeterFly feed and added a few to the Northside High Theater one as well. I tucked my phone into my cardigan pocket and started to dry another cupcake tin, wiping each section carefully.

"The Wall of Fame is awesome," Izzy said, squinting her eyes at a design she was attempting.

"I hope so. I don't know how much good it will do," I said, as the thought occurred to me that what I'd said about Brie wasn't much different than what was done to the girls on the flyer.

"My mom says sometimes we can only blunder ahead and hope what we do will make a difference," Tessa said. "I used to think that was dumb. But now?" She shrugged. "Maybe this is what she means. It would be nice to know something like this would help. But we can't really know ahead of time, can we?"

In the moment that followed, I fully expected Tessa or Izzy to bring up that awful moment where I had blasted my frustration about Brie. When they didn't, I changed the subject. "Okay, girls, I need your incredible wisdom." I told them about Wilson's winky-face text.

"You've been here for thirty minutes, and you're just now telling us that?" Izzy had a huge grin on her face.

"It might not mean anything!" I said.

"Or it might mean everything," Izzy said.

"Do you like him?" Tessa asked. "He's super cute in like a quiet way, you know?"

"I don't know. Maybe?" I honestly didn't want to get my hopes up. All the times Izzy and I talked about the cute boys around us was easy and fun since it was unlikely they would ever speak to me. But Wilson? He was a friend, and that made the possibility more real.

Tessa said, "Just be friends then. Don't overthink it."

"Stars, Tessa. He sent her a winky face!!" Izzy was so excited she squirted green frosting onto the floor.

They laughed, and I joined in, shoving away that hollow, Brie-shaped pit in my stomach.

—⁓—

The next day during Drama 1, I made the rounds to the fundraising groups and verified everyone's work committees. I added to our hashtag feeds and made two trips to the office to get posters.

I brought a stack over to the girls. "Why don't we hang these Sunday when we're downtown? Better yet, maybe we should make a special trip tomorrow."

"Sure," Izzy said.

Shay looked doubtful.

"I'm sorry, I can't help," Tessa said. "I'm leaving school right after class today for State Finals and will be gone until Sunday afternoon. As soon as I get back, I'm supposed to help with the baby." She looked pained at the thought. It still hurt her to see her dad with his girlfriend/soon-to-be wife and their baby. We could tell she loved the little boy but had told us about her wild emotions the few times she had been with them all. "I'll be there right before closing time, though."

"That's okay," I said. "We get it. I haven't heard from Jenna, but I'm going to talk to her in fifth. You guys?"

"Corinna said she would come," Tessa said. "I'm pretty sure our swim team connection made it easier for her to say yes."

"I haven't heard from Fatima, but I'm going to try and say something at rehearsal. Let her know I'm not some crazy person," Shay said.

"Dee said yes but nothing from Selena. I'll talk to her today." I nodded.

"Have any of you checked the Wall of Fame?" Izzy asked. "Someone said I had a great smile! Wait! It wasn't one of you guys, was it?"

We shook our heads.

Izzy pressed her hand to her chest. "It made me feel so good to see that! Not like it wouldn't count if it came from you guys, but that it came from someone else? I feel so . . . full! The Wall is a great idea, Amelia!"

"Help me keep checking it though! I don't want anyone to ruin it by posting something awful, you know?" I said.

"We'll help," Shay promised.

I texted Jenna, Presley, and Brie and asked them to meet me onstage during lunch so that we could talk about the mountain we were tasked to build. They weren't happy about it, but they finally agreed. I hated missing another day of selling cupcakes—especially when they were short Tessa, too, but I knew the mountain had to come first.

The stage was quiet when I got there, with only the ghost light on. As I approached the circle of light center stage, an annoyed voice rang out. "I don't understand why we have to skip lunch for this," Presley was saying as the three girls walked onstage. "We'll have plenty of time to build this thing."

"We really don't. It's not an easy project," I said.

"Then maybe someone else should be on this committee. We're already carrying the whole show," Jenna grumbled. "We have enough going on."

Brie scowled and glared at me.

"Everyone has jobs," I said. "You guys worked on a committee last year, right?"

"Yeah, but we didn't have huge parts in the production," Presley said. "We were assigned to props, which was super simple." She turned to Jenna and Brie. "We should email Ms. Larkin and ask to be reassigned."

"We can't bug Ms. Larkin with this when her mother is so sick," I said. "If we work together, it won't take as long." Then I launched into the instructions Mrs. Lewey had given me. They watched as I hauled out the chicken wire. Brie finally dropped her backpack to the floor, rolled her eyes, and held one end while I cut. Jenna and Presley went to the top of the sets of stairs to fasten the wire at the top.

They complained the entire time—throughout lunch and the beginning of Drama 2. Brie less than the others. At least we got all the chicken wire cut and attached at the top, leaving some of the bottom open so that we could stuff and contour the mountain. We still had twenty minutes of Drama 2 left, but as soon as the last piece was attached, they bailed.

"Brie, wait," I called out. She stopped but didn't turn around right away.

"Is someone else helping you with your lines? I could tell Ken—"

"Leave me alone," she snapped and walked off.

—⁃∞⁃—

"She doesn't want me to help," I repeated to Kenny that afternoon. "I can't force her."

Kenny wasn't having it. "Then you have to convince her. Being in leadership means guiding people even when they don't want to be guided."

Yeah. Well. How do you guide a donkey that refuses to budge?

"Run lines with her! Practice!" He lowered his voice and leaned toward me. "Every day I have someone complain about her. Cast members are going to Mrs. Rinaldi, too. Have you seen how they look at Peter? They're getting hostile. It's causing the whole atmosphere to be toxic."

"Do you think some of it is because they haven't caught who-ever did the flyers?" I looked pointedly at Dev and Hayden, who were having a private contest juggling various props.

Kenny huffed. "Frankly. No. Been in the business too long. It's Peter bringing us down. Plain and simple. And it's got to stop. Do something, stage manager." He threw me a meaningful look indicating that was all he was going to say about it.

I had to admit, he was probably right. Even with the Wall of Fame, rehearsal had a growing negative vibe—especially when Brie was onstage needing lines. She couldn't even get through the Act 1 nursery scenes, which we had rehearsed countless times. It had to be embarrassing because she was obviously the only one struggling.

Theresa McDonald came up to me during a break. She was also a junior like Jenna and her friends but tended to hang with a much quieter group of girls. She played Mrs. Darling, which was kind of perfect for her. She had a motherly feel and was one of the few who always stayed focused and respectful of the whole rehearsal process.

"Would it be rude for me to offer to help Brie with her lines?" Theresa asked. She looked over at where Brie was talking with Jenna—and not looking at her lines. I rolled my eyes.

"I don't think it's rude, but she seems pretty sensitive about it." I shrugged. "I've been trying. It can't hurt to offer." I would *so* prefer that Theresa help Brie.

"Oh well, if you're trying, that's good. That makes me feel better. As long as she's getting help," she said and walked away, taking with her my golden opportunity of giving the job to someone else.

Kenny called rehearsal back to order.

For the next hour, I watched Brie carefully, trying to figure out the problem. When it came to the physical stuff, she was on point. She moved great and was always right where she was supposed to be. But the lines eluded her.

I waited until after rehearsal to corner her again. She was sliding her water bottle into her backpack when I caught her.

She scowled even before I said anything.

"Look. I get it. You don't want my help. But Kenny is insisting, and he's the director." I lowered my voice. "Brie, you don't want to mess up your lines in front of an audience, do you?"

I couldn't read her face. I didn't know her very well, but if I had to guess, she looked somewhere between screaming at me and bursting into tears.

"I'm sure you've been trying," I said. Even though I was not convinced that was the case. "Let me at least run lines with you."

She was quiet for a long minute. So long that I wondered if she was going to answer at all.

"When?" she asked.

"Now?" I asked. "We can stay here for a while."

She sighed loud and long, then dropped her bag. "Fine."

I grabbed my binder and sat in the center of the stage. "Let's start at the beginning."

She sat down cross-legged in front of me and closed her eyes.

Apologize, apologize, my heart urged. But I was too embarrassed. And I finally had her here, willing to run lines. I didn't want her running off like the last time I tried to apologize.

I read Wendy's dialogue. The exchange between the two characters was supposed to be a quick conversation. But Brie simply couldn't do it. Over and over I gave her the line. I could tell she was getting super frustrated—and so was I.

"Okay. That's good for today," I said, even though we had gotten nowhere. I knew Kenny wouldn't be satisfied with today's attempt. Especially since it hadn't helped. "Why don't we meet every day. Which do you prefer—before or after rehearsal?"

"After, I guess." And she walked off. No thank-you, no nothing.

And no apology from me. I winced.

Before I left, I scanned the notes on the Wall of Fame, feeling warm about the many nice comments. Then I froze. On one of the Post-its someone had written "Brie is gonna ruin the show!" I snatched it off and crumpled it. If we didn't come up with a solution soon, I was afraid the note would become reality.

Chapter
23

SATURDAY MORNING I woke up way earlier than I needed to and spent twice as much time getting ready as I usually did. I finally settled on some red plaid pants and a long-sleeved vintage T-shirt. It was getting warmer outside, so I didn't throw on a cardigan, but I did choose a mustard-colored beanie. I studied myself in the mirror. *Was my outfit too weird for Aspire?* It's how I always dressed for school, but I had no idea what Aspire kids would be like. I typically looked a little weird at my youth group. *Would they be youth-group-type kids?*

I decided that, at the very least, I had to feel like myself.

I was nervous. I didn't mind meeting new people in general, but I didn't like going into a situation where I was the only new person.

Wilson would be there though. *Winky-face Wilson.* I pushed away the thought. Nope. Not letting myself go there. He was becoming a good friend, and I really liked that. It didn't need to be complicated. I wouldn't let it get complicated.

Aspire practiced at a church near the downtown mall where

Shay lived above the bookstore. My mother dropped me off at a corner nearby after asking me three thousand times if I was going to be okay. Maybe it was because I was the baby of the family, but it sometimes seemed like she didn't believe I could do anything on my own. She told me to text her when I was finished and thankfully didn't ask any more questions about Wilson.

Volunteering was very important to my parents. So me working as a volunteer should be something they'd want to encourage. Whether this would help me when I asked to audition in the fall, I didn't know. It couldn't hurt. One step at a time.

Although it was chilly, the sun was out. It was starting to feel like spring. Buds on the trees and birds chirping. Being a few blocks from Shay made me realize I hadn't told my friends I was going to check out Aspire.

I found the church halfway down the block. When I couldn't figure out which door to go in, I texted Wilson.

While I waited, I texted Jenna.

Me: Would love for you to come tomorrow night at 8 to meet with the other girls. At Booked Up.

I looked at my phone. *What more could I say to convince her?*

Me: You're not alone in this.

I was worried about her. So for the first time in a while, I prayed for someone else. Praying for her felt different than praying about my own stuff. I hoped God would hear a prayer for Jenna.

I heard a side door open and turned to see Wilson beckoning me. As I moved toward him, I tried not to focus on his lips or attempt to read his eyes. I was there to experience Aspire, not analyze my relationship with Wilson.

I expected to enter a room filled with focused and driven students led by a team of professionals. I imagined everyone sitting studiously, scripts open, taking notes. Silence as the director spoke. Sets right out of a Broadway show.

I walked into . . . chaos.

The rehearsal space was essentially a church basement with chairs and tables pushed to the side. A distinct smell of garlic and spaghetti wafted from the kitchen. There were a bunch of loud little kids running around, shrieking, while a handful of adults gathered in a corner by an electric piano, out of the fray. A group of little boys chased and tackled one another. A group of young girls clustered around plastic boxes were drawing on the lids with markers. There were some teens scattered about the room.

I cringed, and Wilson laughed.

"Lots of energy here," he said. "Let me introduce you to Peggy."

He took me to the group of adults and stepped up to an older woman with short gray hair and a no-nonsense attitude. "Peggy? This is my friend Amelia. She's a drama student, and she's interested in Aspire. I suggested she come volunteer with me, so she can see what it's all about."

"Hi, Amelia. Welcome. The more the merrier," Peggy said, waving her hand to indicate the chaos around us. She looked at Wilson. "Is she going to tech with you?"

Wilson shrugged. "If that's best."

"Would that work for you?" Peggy asked me, a warm smile replacing the no-nonsense impression.

I nodded. Working tech would at least put me with Wilson. Not that that was super important or anything.

Peggy nodded. "Feel free to hang out and watch. The more you know the flow of the show, the easier it will be to become a part of us. Welcome aboard."

"Thanks."

I hoped I wasn't making a commitment to get on board before

checking out the train and making sure it was okay with my parents.

Wilson and I moved to the side as Peggy called for the room to come to order. And to her credit, most of it did. There were a few wriggly younger boys and girls, but they seemed to settle overall.

Although he didn't know everyone, Wilson pointed out some of the teenagers he knew. "During a break I'll introduce you," he whispered.

They were blocking the Munchkinland scene when Dorothy first arrives. I liked Peggy. She was serious, knew what she was doing and what she expected. She gave directions in that firm, no-nonsense tone I'd suspected in the beginning—but without being harsh or condescending.

The girl who played Glinda responded, "Yes, ma'am," anytime Peggy gave her direction. And she knew her lines. At least for the scene they were doing.

The kids were a little nutty. Even though I babysat a lot, it was rarely more than three at a time. When I looked at the website, I hadn't understood that Aspire included a mass of elementary school kids. But even though they were a bit nutty, they still listened. Mostly.

I didn't notice the apathy I sensed at school. There was more excitement here. More anticipation.

I liked it.

After some preliminary tech stuff, Wilson expertly gave me instructions on what and how to set up for the rehearsal; we sat against a wall to observe and make notes on what might need adjustment. Our legs were splayed out, and he was close, leaning over to whisper or point things out.

I told myself to ignore the little fluttery feelings.

Wilson was my friend.

Flutter. Flutter.

As I watched, I wished that I was part of this production too.

Even though it was already cast, it would be fun being part of this energy, this excitement—at any level. *You will be*, I reminded myself. *By summer camp, if not before.* A thrill swept through me. I could hardly believe it. When *Peter Pan* ended, I wouldn't have to wait nearly a year to be part of another show!

Thoughts of gratitude overflowed, thankful Wilson had invited me to come. Volunteering to see what Aspire was like had never occurred to me.

I turned my attention to Adriana, the girl who played Glinda. She was really good. She was a great singer and had a warmth to her as she spoke to the munchkins and patted them on the head. I couldn't help comparing the ease with which she spoke her lines to Brie's struggle. I had no idea what to do. Feeding her every line during the show was not an option. *So what was?*

When they broke for lunch, Wilson took me to Adriana and a couple of other girls from the ensemble. He very awkwardly, but sweetly, introduced me and then promptly disappeared.

They invited me to sit with them to eat lunch. I looked around for Wilson but didn't see any sign of him. I hoped he hadn't ditched me completely.

"You do tech stuff?" Adriana asked.

"Not usually. But maybe for this show. I would rather act. I wanted to audition, but my parents said no."

She was sitting cross-legged eating noodles out of a Tupperware container. She nodded. "It took me forever to convince my parents to let me audition for a show."

"Really?"

"Yeah. It took some begging and some help from Grandma." She laughed and rubbed her thumb against her fingers indicating "money." "Once I started, that's all I wanted to do. *Wizard* is my seventh show. I literally don't do anything else." She laughed again, and a few of the girls around her nodded in agreement.

I smiled yet also felt a bit intimidated. *Seven shows with Aspire already?* And she was genuinely talented. She'd be very hard to compete with.

"What year are you?" I asked.

"Sophomore. I go to Summit Christian."

I had heard of Summit. "Are a lot of these kids from Summit?"

"Not really," she said, glancing at the groups of kids eating picnic style on the floor. "Public schools, private schools, homeschool. Some of everyone here."

I didn't recognize anyone from my school, but Northside was fairly large, so there could be someone here I didn't know.

"Tell me about casting," I said. "Is it hard to get a lead if you haven't been a part of an Aspire production before?" I figured I'd come right out and ask. *Why not?* I needed to know if a real part was a possibility.

Adriana shrugged. "It's hard to say. It depends on the show and who they need. They've had first-timers get leads, and there are others who've done more shows than me and have never gotten a lead. It seems they cast based on what will create the best show possible. We're doing it for God, after all. He deserves our best." Adriana's expression said her words were genuine.

"Of course," I said. *He deserves our best.*

I felt like a fake sometimes. I absolutely believed in God. There was never a moment of my life when God wasn't a part of it. That wasn't the issue. *But others seemed to do the Christian thing . . . better than me somehow? More naturally?* It was like I was sitting on the side of the pool with my feet dangling in the water but hadn't jumped all the way in. I didn't even know why, but it seemed Adriana and the girls, and even Wilson, were clearly swimming, and I wasn't.

They finished lunch, and I thanked Adriana for her honesty. I went looking for Wilson, and when I couldn't find him, I wandered to a table in the back of the room where some moms were sewing.

I wasn't ready to leave but didn't relish the idea of just standing around. "Can I help with something?" I asked.

"Have a seat. Join the fun!" An older woman with soft wrinkles and silvery hair beckoned me over. She was bigger, like me, and she had a nice smile. "I'm Amara," she said. "I'm . . ." She looked around the rehearsal room. "Well, my granddaughter's out there somewhere, but I can't see her right now." She laughed, nice and loud. "Can you sew?"

I laughed. "Absolutely not!"

"Well, I'll teach you then." Amara held up a small garment. "These are the monkey vests. We want them to look like little soldiers." She laughed again. "Of course, the little boys are delighted to not only be a monkey but a soldier as well." While she talked, she took a roll of gold braid, snipped a strip of it, and showed me how to hand sew it to a red vest.

I was clumsy at first, but Amara encouraged me until I got the hang of it. I stitched and listened to the moms talk about the show and the costumes, and once in a while they brought a kid to the table and had them try something on. They asked me some polite questions about my family, my school, and why I was there.

Every so often I looked up from my sewing to watch the rehearsal, surprised that here I was, in the trenches, and happier than I'd been in some time.

Chapter
24

Izzy, Shay, and I met at the bookstore on Sunday afternoon. We each took a stack of *Peter Pan* posters to hang in the downtown area. The shop owners were mostly glad to help. I loved it when they mentioned their intention to bring their kids or that they had already bought tickets.

We ended at the taqueria to down taquitos and guacamole and chips and luscious melted queso, checking our phones for any news from Tessa. She'd won some of her heats and posted a selfie with her swim-team buddy Abraham in their matching swim caps and tagging it #winners. If she kept up this streak, she'd qualify for Nationals in July. We tossed our grease-stained paper boxes in the trash and said our goodbyes, even though we'd meet again in a few hours.

On Sunday evening, I got to Booked Up just as Aunt Laura waved goodbye to the last customer. Zoe was already waiting with Tessa, who looked tired. She had gone straight from the last heat (which she won) in Indianapolis to her father's to help with the baby for a couple of hours while Rebecca had gone to some kind of teacher training.

I had met Zoe briefly at the One Acts last fall and maybe somewhere else I couldn't quite remember. She seemed nice—and must be since Izzy and Tessa adored her. She had an ease about her that made me feel instantly calm. Her black hair was braided into multiple-sized braids and swept up on top of her head. She wore jeans with a tunic-style top and a beautiful jade-colored necklace. My youth group leader, on the other hand, had a dad bod and a beard and thought playing basketball in the parking lot was a solid activity choice for everyone. I was pretty sure if Zoe were my youth group leader, I'd probably like it more. Everything about her seemed warm.

Dee and Corinna both showed up looking cautious. Corinna had the same athletic build as Tessa and silky black hair that went past her shoulders. Dee was a tiny cheerleader, her dark brown skin flawless and her makeup perfect.

"Is anyone else coming?" Zoe asked.

"Fatima said she'd be a little late," Shay said.

"Selena can't come," Izzy said.

I went to check my phone to see if Jenna had texted and realized I left it in Mom's car. Figures. I stepped outside the door to look. Jenna was standing out in front of Grounds and Rounds with a coffee and her phone. I hurried over to her. "I'm so glad you came!"

Jenna gave me a tight smile and stayed put. "I haven't *come* anywhere yet."

"True. But it's right there. Just a few steps away." I pointed to the bookstore. "You'll love Zoe."

"Zoe?" Jenna sipped her coffee.

"She's a youth group leader."

"Like from a church?" she said flatly.

I nodded. "Yep. She's cool, I promise. If you hate it, you can leave whenever."

Jenna shrugged slightly, but that was enough for me.

"Let's go!"

Jenna silently followed me inside and nodded when everyone was introduced. We took the group to the alcove where everyone found a seat. I was instantly grateful for Zoe. If she hadn't been there, I didn't know what we would say.

Zoe started without hesitation. "I've heard about what happened at the high school, and I know the authorities are dealing with parts of it. But"—Zoe pressed her hand to her chest and composed herself—"you girls are the ones on my heart. All the girls who found themselves trapped in the middle of this. I don't like to use the word *victims* because that makes you sound helpless. You aren't helpless. You have great value and worth, and no one, not anyone, can take that from you. That power is in your hands."

I looked at the four girls, and I could tell that, although they were quiet, the words were meaningful to them.

Before the girls had arrived, Zoe suggested that Shay, Tessa, and I only stay for the first part since we weren't directly affected. So we got up to leave. But I decided to say what was on my heart. "I think you are incredibly brave, and I'm glad you came. We wanted to make sure that you know we are here for you in any way we can be."

We left to give them some privacy and ended up having a session of our own with Aunt Laura in the front of the bookstore.

"How's the new baby?" Aunt Laura asked Tessa.

"He's fine. He pretty much sleeps right now. Occasionally he looks at you like he can't quite process what he's seeing." She took out her phone and showed us pictures. None of us present were really "baby people," so we didn't ooh and ahh and coo about how darling he was. He was . . . well . . . a baby.

"Newborns are so ugly," Shay said, then slapped her hand over her mouth. "I'm sorry!" she said from behind her hand.

Tessa burst out laughing.

"Shay!" exclaimed Aunt Laura, who was clearly trying not to laugh.

"Thank you, Shay, for being honest," Tessa said, still laughing. "You've made my day." Shay's honesty seemed to give Tessa permission to be truly honest about her conflicting emotions and even resentment and anger toward Logan. "It's so hard. It's not his fault that any of this happened, but it still hurts, you know?" Tessa said. "When I hold him and look into his tiny face, I melt because he's my brother. But then I hand him back to Rebecca and my stomach flip-flops, and all I can think of is getting out of there."

We let her talk and pretty much listened.

It crossed my mind that maybe I could bring up the entire Brie situation and get help finding a solution. But then I would have to bring up my shameful moment of blurting out what Ms. Larkin had told me in secret. My emotions had bubbled up so quickly in that moment that I had let them come spilling out unchecked. I was well aware that my emotions, like everything else in my life, were big. I didn't see myself as unstable, but I wondered if I might feel everything more powerfully than other people. More than my family members for sure. I had learned to turn down my emotions some, but the feelings were still bigger than me at times. And that's when I said or did something I completely regretted.

I was still contemplating whether to bring it up when Zoe emerged with the other girls, their eyes glistening with tears. I hoped they were good tears.

Zoe gave each girl a big hug and reminded them that God saw them and cared for them and to text her anytime. Knowing that Zoe was available to them took an enormous load off me. *I mean, goodness. What did I know? I wasn't a counselor.* What was I supposed to say that would help them process the entire mess?

I used Tessa's phone to text Mom to come get me. Shay and Aunt Laura escorted us to the sidewalk in front of the store where we said our goodbyes, and then they dipped back in to lock up.

When the others had gone, Jenna still lingered. I waited in silence, feeling a bit awkward. After a moment, Jenna gestured toward the bookstore and spoke. "You were right about Zoe. She's pretty cool."

"You think? I don't really know her. But she seems to be. From what I hear from Izzy and Tessa, I'm guessing she's serious about texting her whenever."

Jenna smirked. "Yeah. I got that impression."

Mom pulled up. "There's my ride," I said.

"Wait." Jenna closed her eyes and took a deep breath. She opened them and looked right at me. "Thanks for texting me this week."

"Oh sure, anytime!" I said.

"No. I mean, it helped a lot. I was in a . . . really dark place. You were the only one who reached out to me."

"Really?"

Jenna nodded. "Yeah. But with your texts and this," she said, waving at the store, "life doesn't feel as dark."

—⁊⁊—

On Monday I got permission to go spend time with the mountain during Drama 1 and found wrestling the chicken wire into place oddly satisfying.

What I'd said about Brie to Tessa and Izzy was true, but blurting out truth wasn't always wise. I remember when I was in middle school, I was justifying something I'd said. I had told Mom I was "just being honest."

Mom had said, "You know, telling the truth and being a truthful person are good things. But there is such a thing as discretion.

And a truthteller needs to also know when to be silent and when to speak and how to speak. Jesus was full of truth *and* grace."

It took me a while to mull that over and understand it. Sometimes grace meant we kept our mouths shut. *And this time?* I had put up the Wall of Fame to bring people together, and with my big mouth, I'd accomplished the exact opposite and blown them apart.

I picked through the pile of recyclables for stuff to shape the mountain. Bits of cardboard and paper. Other people's trash to be reused. Repurposed. Made new. Their usefulness restored—just in a different way than before.

I worked the pieces underneath the wire to create the contours and rocky outcroppings of a mountain, one agonizing section at a time. I wasn't alone there on the stage. There were others there too. But I was deaf to their conversations. As far as I was concerned, it was just the three of us—me, my thoughts, and the mountain. Whenever left alone with my thoughts, they always took me back to my expectations that *Peter Pan* would be a magical experience. It wasn't magical. It was a disappointment. Not getting the role I'd dreamed of was a disappointment. Being a pirate was a disappointment. Seeing the apathy of the cast was a disappointment. Watching the chosen Peter flop heightened my disappointment. Being a stage manager was great work and suited me well. But that role didn't make my disappointments disappear.

I had dreamed of being onstage, front and center, and yet on opening night I'd spend most of my time out of sight.

I crumpled a stack of three-hole-punched seminar notes into big balls and tried not to scratch myself on the chicken wire, yet again, as I found a place to tuck them underneath it. Those seminar notes must have mattered at some point. But now they were trash. Suitable only as mountain guts.

I had kept telling myself that my role as a pirate didn't matter. Just a throwaway part. No one would notice me in my stupid balloon-blouse and balloon-pants.

That really wasn't true, though, was it? When I sat in the front row of the auditorium next to Kenny, he often barked to a Lost Boy or an Indian who wasn't paying attention. It didn't take long to see what he saw. I began to recognize that anyone in the audience would be able to tell who was engaged in the scene and who wasn't. Kenny pointed out how the expressions on the face of every person onstage absolutely mattered. You never knew where the audience would look. If you weren't committed to the scene, people noticed.

—m—

I worked through lunch. At the beginning of Drama 2, after I checked in with the sub, I went to The Trio made up of Jenna, Presley, and Brie. "Just thought I'd let you know I'm working on the mountain if you want to come help."

Jenna threw up her hands, looking like that little shrugging emoji. "Sorry. I have makeup work from last week."

"The 'Ugg-a-Wugg' dance number is calling my name," Presley said. "There are a few Indians who need extra practice."

I looked at Brie, but she stared at the script lying open in her lap.

I went back to the auditorium to continue working on the mountain by myself. While trying to maneuver a tricky piece of cardboard into place, the chicken wire broke free from its mooring and sprung back at me. I grabbed it, cutting my finger in the process. I held it tight, but little drops of blood marked my way to find a paper towel to wrap around it. I held the paper tight around my throbbing finger as the blood made a large red spot on the paper towel.

When I turned around, the mountain didn't look like much. The bottom corner gave me a little glimpse of what the whole thing might look like once it was finished. *If* it ever got finished. There was so much left to do.

I sat down, cross-legged, and stared at it. I was overwhelmed. My finger hurt. The mountain loomed. My heart hurt. My emotions bloomed. And I finally allowed myself to admit the reality of my situation. I knew why I resented being a pirate. I knew why it seemed impossible to help Brie.

I was mad.

I was mad because I didn't get my way.

I was the little kid throwing a tantrum because she didn't get what she wanted. Mad as a hornet at the One who said no.

I moved a clean part of the paper towel over my wound and squeezed harder.

Why couldn't this one huge, important thing have worked out the way I wanted it to? Why couldn't God have said yes to this one little request? And why did this feel so wildly unfair?

"Yo. Smee," came a deep voice from somewhere behind a curtain.

"Yeah?"

"Can you bring me some of that black paint? I've got a dripping paintbrush and nowhere to put it down."

"Aye, aye, Cap'n Hook."

"Knock it off."

"Dude. You started it."

"You remind me of Cap'n Crunch."

"You remind me of Sméagol."

I had to laugh. This kind of banter was one of the reasons I loved theater, and here I was letting my own pride keep me from enjoying every moment to the fullest. Me. Amelia Bryan, the girl who could have fun anywhere, make fun everywhere, had let her own stubbornness keep her from embracing all of it.

Where had I taken that left-hand turn?

I pressed my palms on the floor, bloody paper towel and all. Closed my eyes to really feel the stage underneath me. This world fit me in a way no other one did. I was a real and vital part of it. It was a real and vital part of me. To fully grow, I had to accept this show for what it was. Not the version I had invented and anticipated for months. That version did not exist.

Smee and Captain Hook continued their banter in the background as they worked on the pirate ship, and in that moment, I decided that even if I couldn't change the hollow feeling deep within, I could choose to embrace the entirety of *Peter Pan*— exactly as it was. I would make it the best show possible because I wanted to, not because I thought that was my only choice or to gain some nebulous thing in the future.

I would start with the mountain.

I didn't get very far before rehearsal, but I was nothing if not determined. Putting my effort into the mountain was easy compared to having to face the damage I'd caused the show. It would be good to talk with Izzy, Shay, and Tessa, but I was too ashamed.

As Kenny worked on the final blocking for the last nursery scene, he flashed me a look every time Brie needed a line. Like it was my fault.

When Brie stopped yet again, I opened my mouth to feed her the line, but Gabby Arnold, one of the Lost Boys, yelled into the quiet space, "If you didn't want the part, why are you even here?"

The entire room stilled. But Gabby, now that she had started, seemed unable to stop. "You're gonna ruin the show for everyone. You should've quit!"

Brie froze. Kenny stared at her openmouthed. Heads nodded in agreement.

It was like a gaping hole had opened up in the side of my boat, and words from the cast rushed out like a flood.

"We open in two weeks!"

"She can't do it!"

"Let someone else be Peter!"

But I was the one who'd started that hole. I looked at Brie. Her face was pinched. She was trembling. I did this to her. *Why had I been so angry with her?* Brie hadn't taken anything away from me because the part was never mine to begin with.

It wasn't my part.

It was hers.

I realized, all of a sudden, that I had heard Ms. Larkin wrong. Brie was *nervous* about taking the part. Ms. Larkin had said she lacked confidence. That wasn't the same thing as not wanting *to be* Peter.

"Stop it!" I shouted. "It's not true that she didn't want the part! Ms. Larkin chose her for a reason. We have to trust that Ms. Larkin knew what she was doing."

Everyone fell silent.

"It's a rumor that Brie didn't want to play Peter. I know it's a rumor because it came from something I said. Ms. Larkin told me—as the stage manager—some information in confidence. I took it out of context and in frustration and anger blurted it to someone else. I messed up—as a stage manager, as a castmate, as a . . . as a friend."

I thought about adding how I hadn't intended for anyone else to hear, but that didn't matter. The boat was sinking, and it was my fault. "We have to fully support one another for this show to be all that it can be. And right from the start, I didn't do that." I turned to Brie. "I'm sorry, Brie. I'm really sorry for"—I made myself say it—"being so jealous of you that I have never supported you as Peter."

Brie stared at me, and I couldn't read her expression.

I turned back to the cast. "Listen up, everyone. This negative attitude toward Brie has to stop. Brie is Peter. She's going to be an awesome Peter. Ms. Larkin believed in her. We have to, too. I believe in you, Brie."

I clapped, slowly, like in the show when Peter turns and asks the audience to clap if they believe in fairies. I didn't have to explain it to the cast. They knew exactly what I was doing, and one by one, they joined in. A few even shouted, "I believe in you, Brie!"

Brie, who had stood frozen, suddenly bolted from the stage. Kenny smirked at me. "I hope you have a plan."

I did not.

———◆◆◆———

I went looking for Brie. After a good ten minutes I finally spotted her in the back corner of the band room behind a drum set.

She was crying. And it was my fault.

She was a person with feelings, and I had treated her badly—like an object. I'd had no patience or empathy for her because I was jealous. I listened enough in church to know that jealousy ruined things. People. Relationships. Jealousy was cruel. I wasn't a cruel person, but I had been cruel to her from the beginning—for no other reason than she got the part I wanted.

I felt like a horrible person. Truly horrible.

I went over to where she was sitting against the wall, knees pulled up to her chest and arms wrapped around them.

I sat on the ground in front of her. "I'm sorry. I'm sorry for treating you badly. For not helping you the way I should have. I hope you can forgive me—even though I absolutely don't deserve it."

She raised her chin to look at me, eyes red. They'd be puffy soon. "But you're right. I'm terrible at Peter." She focused on the floor. "I work on those lines constantly," she muttered.

I didn't say anything because, had she really been working hard to memorize them?

"I'm dyslexic." She said it so quietly, I barely heard her. "The words. They get stuck and turned around—" She stopped abruptly and pressed her lips together.

Now I felt even worse. I had been wrong about everything.

"I'm sorry," I said again. "For judging you. For speaking a confidence I had no right to share—and saying it loud enough for others to hear. For not truly caring about you."

Brie continued to stare at the floor, large tears dropping onto her shoes.

"I meant what I said in there. Ms. Larkin believed that you'd be the best Peter. And I do too," I said. "Actually, you will be an amazing Peter."

In that moment, I sensed God giving me compassion for her. Like once I was willing to take off the glasses of jealousy I wore, He could give me a new perspective. I genuinely wanted to help her.

"I shouldn't have even tried out," Brie said. "I tried to tell Ms. Larkin in the beginning, but she talked me into it. Said that I would be fine. But I'm not fine. I'm going to ruin the show."

I put my hands on my hips and looked sternly at her. "You're not. We're going to figure this out, okay? But you have to let me help you."

"I don't know how you can. I've tried everything," she said, tears slipping down her face.

"We're not going to give up. Even if I have to lie under a rug onstage and give you every line, I will."

Brie snorted and then smiled a little. "Okay," she whispered.

Chapter
25

WE SLIPPED BACK into rehearsal. The tension hadn't dissipated. Some people scowled at me, while most turned away. Izzy and Tessa gave me sad smiles.

I deserved it. I was a hypocrite. Waving my hands around saying we should support one another when I was throwing Brie overboard.

Even as I continued feeding lines to Brie throughout the rest of rehearsal, I felt awful. I couldn't undo the damage I had done. Even though half of the people in the cast had surely gossiped about someone, it was like I was the only one who had earned the scarlet letter *G* pinned to my chest.

I bolted after rehearsal. I didn't want to talk to anyone, especially the Fan4.

When Mom picked me up, she told me she needed me to babysit. I appreciated the distraction. When I heard the Burfield family arrive upstairs, I put the *Seussical* album on the turntable, hoping it would cover any potential arguing from Jon and Leah.

The three girls tumbled downstairs, and even Parker appeared to be in a decent mood. They spent the first ten minutes hugging Felix and playing with him. He acted like it was the most fun he ever had in his life.

"We're going to see *Peter Pan*!" Emma yelled and spun around.

"Mom said you're in it," Parker said.

Ainsley put her arms out and pretended to fly around the room. "Look! I'm flying!"

I laughed.

"I am in it. And Peter really is going to fly!" I picked up Emma and zoomed her around behind Ainsley.

"I want to go! Right now!"

They all talked at once about how excited they were to go to the show and what they would see. And the flying! They were so excited about the flying!

"Do you know who Peter Pan is?" I asked them.

"He flies!" Emma said.

I laughed again, and Felix barked.

"He does! Do you want to hear the story?"

All three girls nodded, eyes wide. "Okay! First we have to make a little house like the Indians live in!" We piled cushions and blankets to make the best tepee we could. I turned off the music and turned on a crackling fire YouTube video. The girls crawled inside our tepee while I sat at the entrance.

"Once upon a time, there was boy who didn't want to grow up . . ."

I told them the whole story, dramatically of course, complete with voices and excitement during the battles. The girls were entranced.

Those faces. That's what all of this was for. They didn't understand leads or roles or ensembles. They didn't care that I was just a pirate. They were simply excited to hear a story. To see a boy fly.

When I finally got back to my room, I went about getting

ready for bed. I tossed my beanie on the floor and looked in the mirror as I combed out my short hair.

Amelia Bryan. Pirate. I growled at the mirror. I twisted myself into different body positions. Maybe my character got stabbed in the left arm during a battle, and it doesn't work properly. Or *her* arm. I didn't have to be a boy pirate. Yes! I'm a female pirate, and my left arm hangs useless by my side. I ran away from home when the love of my life was killed by a warring band of pirates, so now I'm hunting them across the seas! I walked around my room, growling and letting my left arm dangle.

Practice makes perfect.

The sub in Drama 1 immediately sent us out to work on our committees, so I barely got to say hello to my friends. "See you at lunch!" Izzy called out before being swept away with the others for some prop building in another room.

The cafeteria featured burritos for lunch. I swear it was like a hug from God. Burritos made everything better.

The girls were already at the table. I set my tray at my usual place and said, without really looking at anyone, "They have burritos!" As though yesterday hadn't happened. I took my first bite of heaven and chewed slowly.

"You okay?" Shay asked.

"Of course, why?"

The three of them gave me a look. When we first became friends, we had decided to always be real and talk honestly—even about the tough stuff, not letting one another closet our junk. I honestly loved that about them, but it made it much harder to hide. And now, they were waiting, not willing to let me skip this one.

I wiped my hands on the napkin in my lap. "I still feel awful that I blasted about Brie to you guys. And worse, not trying harder to apologize to Brie. I kinda hoped it would just go away. Of course, it didn't, and just because I confessed doesn't mean everything has been fixed."

"Yikes." Shay cringed. "I so get that."

"Yeah. Wow." Izzy looked sympathetic.

"We all make mistakes, Amelia," Tessa said. "I have sure made a few with my dad these past few months."

"Yes, but I somehow managed to make one big enough to sabotage the whole show." I don't know what it was about talking to the Fan4, but it seemed like the deepest parts of my emotions bubbled to the surface more quickly around them. And here they came. Shame. Helplessness. I pleaded with myself not to cry.

Tessa snorted. "You didn't sabotage the whole show. You seem to have forgotten about the flyers that got us off on a bad start even before you announced Brie's issue."

Izzy dropped her own burrito onto her plate and wiped her hands. She leaned in and said, "On that note, turns out Dev and Hayden didn't have anything to do with the flyers. But they do know who did and were covering for him."

"Really? How do you know?" Shay asked.

Izzy froze. Covered her mouth and looked around. "Oops."

"What?" Shay asked, looking around as well.

"I wasn't supposed to say anything," Izzy hissed. She rolled her eyes. "Guess we all blurt out stuff we shouldn't," Izzy said, looking ashamed.

I appreciated her attempt to make me feel better, but that little slip of the tongue was spoken in a low voice and told to a group of girls who would absolutely not tell anyone. Not that it made it okay for her to say. It wasn't. But I had crowed mine at the top of my voice in an echoing auditorium and caused major damage.

"Because I told you that much, I'll also tell you this: It wasn't somebody in the cast."

I breathed a sigh of relief, as though I had been holding it since the day the flyers came out.

"The guy wasn't even related to the Dropbox scandal. It was some freshman kid I've never heard of."

"Huh?" Tessa said. "Then why? How'd he get the names?"

"He was a good listener. He wanted the guys to think he was cool. Didn't work."

"I'm telling you," Shay said. "Teen boys can be idiots."

Tessa tipped her head, a playful smirk coming to her face. "Not all."

"Like Alex," I teased.

"And Wilson," Tessa teased right back.

I blushed. Everyone else laughed.

"Yeah, they're the good guys," Izzy said with a melancholy sigh. I wondered if she was wondering why her crush, Zac, hadn't turned out to be one of the good guys.

We paused for a moment, each occupied with our own thoughts.

"I'm so glad it wasn't a cast member," I said, breaking the silence. Then shame filled my cheeks again, realizing I had falsely accused Dev and Hayden of being responsible.

"How are you doing with Brie?" Tessa asked.

I shook my head.

"Is there anything we can do?" Shay asked.

"I wish. I googled everything about memorizing lines last night . . . and we've tried all of them. Nothing has worked. Frankly, I need a miracle," I said.

"Well, I don't know about getting a *miracle*," Tessa said. "But you could ask God for wisdom."

Would God give me ideas to help Brie if I asked Him? Even though I was disappointed with Him? And made a wreck of things because of my anger and jealousy?

Izzy grinned. "I agree. Let's pray!"

So they prayed for me. Right there in the middle of the

cafeteria. They prayed that I would have wisdom to know how to help Brie. But when they were done, I was disappointed. I don't know what I expected. I guess I'd hoped that some amazing solution would explode in my brain. "Thanks," I said.

Just then, Wilson walked by. "Hey, Amelia," he said, throwing me one of his crooked grins. "It was good to hang out with you this weekend."

"Yeah," I said, unable to come up with anything even a bit more interesting. Once he was gone, they turned to stare at me.

"Ooooooh, girl," Izzy said, drawing out the words. "You've got some 'splainin' to do."

"He invited me to volunteer at Aspire this weekend," I said in a rush and took my last bite of burrito. I could feel the heat rising in my cheeks.

"Stars! I need more details!" Izzy said. She put both her hands under her chin like she was settling in for a story.

"He's a friend!"

Flutter.

Tessa raised an eyebrow at me. The others had similar "yeah, sure" expressions.

I wiped my hands and wadded up the napkin. "There's nothing more to tell. I promise."

"But . . ." Shay said.

"You like him?" Izzy asked, shimmying her shoulders with a grin on her face.

Tessa nodded. "She likes him."

"No! I don't know. Maybe?" I squeaked out that last word, and my voice was about two octaves higher than normal.

Flutter.

"It doesn't matter anyway because he hasn't asked to hang out since I said no to the smoothies."

"But he took you to Aspire?" Izzy asked.

"Sort of. I met him there since my parents freaked about a boy driving me anywhere. He volunteers for Aspire and thought volunteering would be a good way for me to start being involved with them as well."

"Did you like it?" Tessa asked.

"I loved it. They're doing *Wizard.* I did some tech, watched for a good bit . . . oh, and learned to sew a little!" I knew I was almost bouncing in my seat. But I couldn't help it. "And more good news: My parents havea agreed to let me go to the Aspire summer camp!"

The girls erupted in cheers, attracting stares from all around us.

"I'm super excited." I leaned forward and lowered my voice, realizing that once again, I had gotten too loud. "But I can't think about it yet. *Peter Pan* comes first, and we owe it to the audience to give them a great show." I thought of Emma's, Ainsley's, and Parker's faces.

"It's going to be a great show," Izzy said.

"Is Peter going to fly?" Shay asked.

"Yep. The company comes in for tech week. But we have to keep up the fundraising momentum in case there are unexpected financial needs."

"Oh, we'll keep going!" Izzy said. "It's been so much fun!"

"I'm sorry I haven't help—"

Izzy waved me off before I could finish. "It's okay. Really."

"It was fun," Tessa said. "But we missed you."

"I wish I could figure out how to help Brie," I said. "If only it were as easy as inviting her to a cupcake-baking party."

"Um, didn't we pray?" Izzy asked.

"You really think God will answer?" I said.

"Uh. Yeah," Izzy said.

I looked at her skeptically.

"Well," said Tessa, "God is the One who made you so creative."

"And smart," Shay said.

"And totally outrageous—in a good way," added Izzy.

In front of me sat three grinning Cheshire Cats.

They saw me that way? I grinned too.

Chapter
26

In Drama 2, Jenna seemed different. Better. I wasn't sure if it was because I saw her differently or if she was less guarded than usual. Or maybe because they caught the flyer guy and she and the other girls didn't have to wonder who it was any longer. Even so, I didn't ask her, Presley, or Brie to help me work on the mountain.

Without the Drama 2 Trio to help me, it was just me and the mountain. I was grateful to be alone with my thoughts, but with all the other cast members there working on sets, it wasn't quiet. It didn't take long, however, before the sounds of hammers and drills and good-natured chatter became shapeless background noise.

I blew out a long sigh and reshaped some cardboard and bubble wrap to make the "rock" jut out more. I sat back and inspected my work. Satisfied with that section, I stapled the bottom of the chicken wire to hold the shaping in place. I decided I liked working on the mountain alone. I found it therapeutic. The mountain and me? We had an understanding.

—〰—

During rehearsals Kenny moved at a lightning pace compared to Ms. Larkin. He was abrupt and could be a little brutal, but he got things done. At Kevon, he'd say, "Boy, you gotta jump like that alligator gonna actually bite you!" At Presley, "Why you trynna look so pretty? You're a warrior!" At Jenna, "You ain't never seen Neverland before. Why you lookin' like you're just walking into school all normal?"

As he called people out on things—big and small—I found myself watching how he directed. He liked movement onstage. Nothing static. It made the scenes feel alive. So much for the audience to see or notice. Each day I could see glimpses of what the show would look like. As the sets and the staging took on color and life, I found myself getting more excited about the show. For real.

Although I had created a fun pirate character for myself, when they did a costume fitting, the sense of how absurd I looked washed over me again. They dressed the pirates, except Hook and Smee, in long black pants that were shredded at the bottom; a dirty white dress shirt shredded at the sleeves; and red, yellow, and black scarves that were tied together and used as belts. We were each given a black bandanna to tie around our heads pirate style. I tried to stick my hair under the bandanna, but that made me look bald. If I left some of my hair out, it created this weird red halo under the bandanna.

Izzy and Tessa were dressed in the costume of the Lost Boys. Their costumes were similar to the pirates'. But theirs had long khaki shorts shredded at the bottom and old ratty T-shirts in a variety of colors. It would have been more fun to be with them for sure, but I reminded myself that being a pirate was part of *Peter Pan*—and some people's favorite part. And I had promised to do my best.

When I wasn't in a scene, I was near my binder, making sure that everyone was hitting their marks. And giving Brie Every. Single. Line.

But as I watched her, I noticed something. If you ignored the line issue, she was good. Expressive. Perky. Always where she needed to be. Never missing a cue. When Kenny discovered her gymnastic abilities, he added a backflip or a cartwheel into every scene possible. And her gymnastics were impressive. When she landed a perfect roundoff, ending with hands on hips Peter-style, I got an idea. She was so good with her body awareness, maybe we could use that to our advantage. I got so excited, I ran up to her the moment rehearsal ended.

"Can you stay today to run lines?" I asked.

She huffed, "Yes. But why bother? Nothing's helping. My parents even hired an acting coach for me to Zoom with. I'm hopeless." She looked so utterly defeated.

"We have to keep at it," I said. "Besides. I have an idea."

She did not look enthusiastic. "I need some stuff from my locker. I'll be back," she said.

"Okay!" I turned and ran into Wilson. Again. Immediately after that embarrassment, I realized I was still in full pirate costume.

"Ahoy, matey!" he said.

"You're hysterical. Truly. Ever consider a career in stand-up?" I said, deflecting my mortification.

"I thought I'd tell you that I'm ready to start focusing on lighting. I'd love to get that part done before tech week," he said.

He gave me a big smile. I felt ridiculous standing there as a pirate. All I wanted to do was go change. "Okay. That's fine. I'm gonna change. I'm rehearsing with Brie. We can keep using the stage, right?"

"Sure. I'll be around for a while in case you need anything," he said.

"Thanks!" I took off to get into my real clothes, and by the time I got back to the stage, Brie was sitting dead center, her face in both hands. It looked like she'd been crying.

"Help me get the nursery set out," I said.

She got up, and we carefully moved everything except the mountain. That took at least five people to move, and it wasn't really in our way.

When we got the nursery scene placed, I climbed up on the window box that was underneath the giant window. "You come in here, right?"

She nodded and pointed out her path. "Then I go there, there, and there."

"And you're calling for Tinker Bell."

She nodded.

"I have an idea. We're going to take each line and give it a physical movement, so when you do that movement, it will help you remember the line."

She scrunched up her nose but then shrugged. "I guess it can't hurt to try."

"Nope! Okay." I pulled out my binder and laid it on Wendy's bed. "Let's walk through the whole scene."

At each mark where she was supposed to give a line, I gave her an action to do while saying the line. Something specific to touch. Stomping. Putting a hand flat on the floor. Opening the drawer. We carefully practiced the line when she was doing the movement. It took a while, and I was worried about how late it was getting, but I kept pushing forward.

After we walked through just the movements and the lines a second time, I said, "Let's try it!"

She looked skeptical. She went to stand where the first line was said, but I sent her to the window. "Start from the beginning. Do the whole thing. Full out."

She climbed up on the box and jumped off, landing quietly in a crouched position. She looked around and went to her first spot. She pulled out the drawer, and after a moment's hesitation said the line on her own. Over and over she'd get to her spot, do the movement, and after a brief pause, say the line. We got to the end of the scene without me having to prompt her once.

I grinned and grabbed her shoulders. "It worked! You did it!"

She looked shocked. "I did, didn't I?"

"Yes! This is going to work! Now we just need to practice so you can find the lines faster and get the scene up to speed."

We went through the scene two more times, and both times she pulled it off. For the first time, I honestly believed she'd be able to do it.

Brie covered her mouth. "What made you decide to try that?"

I shrugged. "Inspiration from God. Seriously. It came to me that your physicality is really strong, so we should try to use your strengths."

She nodded, then walked over and hugged me. "Thank you. Thank you for not giving up on me."

"Thank you for forgiving me and giving me the chance to help," I said. "I'm so proud of you . . . Peter."

The look on her face? Priceless.

—⁂—

After we said excited goodbyes, I went up to Wilson's booth to let him know we were finished.

And to see him.

Wilson was in front of his computer monitor in the dark booth, the screen lighting his face. I knocked on the doorframe since the door was open.

"Oh, hey!" He leaned back in his chair and folded his hands on his belly. "All finished?"

"Yep."

"And?"

"And what?"

"How did it go? I mean, I watch enough rehearsals to know that she's been on the struggle bus."

I grinned. "Yes, but I'm pretty sure we found a way to get her off the bus."

Wilson nodded. "Excellent. Especially since she's literally the whole show."

"Seriously." I glanced at my phone to see what time it was, knowing I should text Mom.

"So tell me what you thought of Aspire. Since we didn't get to talk much."

"Because you ditched me!"

"I didn't mean to ditch you. Honest. Ivan got some new sound equipment, and he wanted to show me. I guess I got distracted by nerd stuff. I'm sorry."

"I'm just messing with you. I hung out with the moms and grandmas and learned to sew. A little anyway."

"Nice. Yes, everyone learns new things at Aspire because everyone has to pitch in and help."

"Well, I loved it. And I get to try the camp! Have you ever helped with those?"

Wilson grinned. "Yep. They always need tech help, so I'll be there."

I smiled back, ignoring the flutters. "I'm excited. But first *Peter Pan*."

Chapter
27

KENNY WAS STANDING CENTER STAGE, Starbucks cup in hand. I ran over to him before I put my backpack down.

"Can we start at the first scene?" I asked.

"Girl, you gotta dial that back about ten notches. I'm still waking up."

"It's two thirty!"

"And?"

"Can we start running from the beginning?" I repeated.

He shrugged. "Nursery's up, so fine with me." He waved at the set. "I hope you got some miracle up your sleeve 'cause otherwise you're gonna be lying under that bed whispering lines the whole show."

If Brie could pull it off after an all-night break, that was a strong indication the method would work. I wanted to run it with her privately, but we didn't have time.

"Places!" Kenny called. "Quiet on the stage."

When Brie jumped into the window of the Darling home, I

sucked in my breath and held it. She jumped down into the squat and looked around. She rushed over to the dresser where she had her first line.

She hesitated, reached out for the drawer, and pulled. A moment passed. Another. Kenny looked at me with an eyebrow up, but I waved at him to give her a second.

Then she said the line.

She went to the closet, reached up and touched the spot we agreed on, and out came the next one.

And on and on. Palms to the floor, and the line came.

A stomp, and the line came.

A thimble up in the air, and the line came.

I wasn't the only one holding my breath. Everyone was watching, still, caught in a moment of awe. Frozen, afraid to move. No one wanted to break the spell.

When she grabbed Wendy's hand and said the final line, the entire cast and crew burst into applause and whistling and stomping.

She did it. She did it!!

Kenny turned to me, put his coffee cup down on the floor, and slow-clapped.

I grinned.

The applause was for Brie, but I took a little of it for me, too. Buoyant excitement filled me. I had a critical hand in someone's success. Brie ran over and hugged me.

"You've got this," I said.

"*We've* got this," she corrected.

She went back to her place, and I looked at Kenny. "We only worked on the first scene, so that's the only miracle you'll witness today!"

Kenny shrugged. "I'll take it. But you will do whatever this was on the rest of the show, right?"

"Absolutely."

As the cast continued to run through the show, I wrote down

ideas for Brie's physical action on each of her lines. I also took notes on props that were in the wrong place. Ideas to make a set change quicker. Tweaking the blocking for better stage balance.

When it was time to change into my pirate costume, I didn't mind. When else was I going to get the chance to stagger around like a drunk, growl at people, and fight?

Everything had shifted, though nothing had changed. Everything felt different. Being at the rehearsal. Watching the rehearsal. Resentment had dimmed my view. But the fog had lifted, and the view was amazing.

After the official rehearsal finished, Brie and I got back to work. The Lost Boy scenes had a lot of people and action, so I was glad for my notes. I had her ruffle the hair of a boy, put her hands on her hips, and other super-specific movements.

It was painstaking work, but Brie was completely focused. Still we only made it partway through Act 1 before she had to leave.

I stayed to worked on the mountain. Watching the sets develop substance was fascinating to me. Wood skeletons nailed to platforms becoming a nursery in London, a pirate ship, a mountain, a magical place called Neverland. The story was coming to life with shape and color. Giant leaves to shelter the Lost Boys. A speckled toadstool big enough to sit on.

I couldn't deny it was magical.

And I was a part of it.

My days became about two things: helping Brie and building the mountain.

The method I had come up with for Brie was an agonizing, tedious process. Learn the physical motions, connect them to a line, practice over and over. She got frustrated. So did I. But we pressed through. Peter needed us both to stay focused on the goal.

The mountain was a bigger problem because the more time I spent with Brie, the less time I had with the mountain. I stayed later and later every evening, but on the Friday afternoon before tech week I knew I was going to have to call for reinforcements.

At lunch, I floated my idea to the girls.

"How would you feel about a lock-in?" I asked. "Tonight."

"A what? What are you talking about?" Tessa said. "You always start in the middle and leave out fifteen thousand details."

"Working with Brie has been very time-consuming and now I've fallen behind on building the mountain. Tech week starts Monday, and it's got to be done before then. I already asked Mrs. Ventrella if we could work onstage Friday after school and stay overnight. We'll be locked inside until Saturday morning."

"That's allowed?" Shay asked.

"We're supposed to keep it quiet. It's not something the school encourages. But for special students and circumstances, they will allow it." I shrugged. "I guess we fit both categories."

"A 'work on the set' sleepover? That sounds like so much fun!!" Izzy said. "I'm texting Papi right now."

"I don't have swim practice until tomorrow afternoon, so it's perfect actually," Tessa said, pulling out her phone.

"I'd have to see if Aunt Laura would be okay with it," Shay said. "But I'm game."

A huge weight lifted off me as my friends texted and chatted with excitement. Surely together we could get the mountain finished.

After rehearsal and a flurry of stops at home to grab snacks, sleeping bags, pillows, hair dryers, and fans, we walked onstage ready to tackle the mountain together. Wilson left lights on for us that lit the stage. *Flutter.* He had kindly added some colored gels so the lights would be softer and more fun. Green. Blue. Red. Yellow. Orange.

"Man," Izzy said, looking above her. "Looks like we've got ourselves a stationary disco ball."

"Earth to Izzy." I pointed to the buckets and the stacks of newspapers. "Time to get dirty."

"Yeah, yeah. One second." She pulled a paint-stained sweatshirt over her T-shirt. "My trusty work shirt," she said, laughing.

Shay tilted her head sideways to take in the different splatters of paint. "I see a newborn baby."

Tessa and I cracked up.

"Huh?" Izzy said.

"You had to be there," Tessa said, still chuckling.

"Well? Where *was* I?"

"Booked Up," Shay said, raising a brow.

"Okay, focus, girls!" I said, clapping twice.

"Yes, Ms. Amelia," Izzy said in a little-girl voice.

Tessa raised her hand. "I have to go wee-wee, Ms. Amelia."

"Oh, stop it," I said, thwacking them both with a rolled-up newspaper. Without shame holding me back, I could enjoy bantering with my friends again.

Everyone sat in front of her own bucket of gloppy papier-mâché and a pile of newspapers. "Take newspaper and begin to rip strips a couple of inches wide. Not that way, Tessa. Turn the newspaper. Now it will rip easily.

"Take your strips and dip them one at a time into the sludge."

"Just like cupcake batter," Izzy said, happily plunging her fingers into the goo.

Shay shivered. "This stuff is just . . . gross. Ugh. It stinks. I don't like how it feels."

"Didn't you ever make a papier-mâché–covered balloon in elementary school?" Tessa asked.

"Uh. No. Now I know the biggest blessing of being homeschooled."

Tessa and Izzy quickly got into the rhythm of dip, squeegee—just the right amount of extra gunk off the strip—and press the strip to the chicken wire.

Shay stared at her bucket for a long minute and then looked up at the mountain that suddenly looked rather enormous from our perspective. "Wow," was all she said.

"You'll get used to it," I said as I set out my little speaker and turned on a peppy Spotify playlist.

I started to paste to the rhythm of the music. "We have to get the mountain completely covered as quickly as possible, overlapping the newspaper enough, but not too thick because we have to dry it and then paint it."

We tore strips, dipped them deep into the buckets, wiped off the excess, and laid them over the chicken wire. We each picked a section of the mountain to work on. Shay took a bucket up the stairs so she could work from the top down.

We sang. We danced with our soggy strips. We laughed.

With the four of us working, we covered the mountain in the first three hours. We set the fans on high and each took a hair dryer. Stationed around the soggy beast, we focused our efforts on the wettest parts. The hair dryers were helping, but it was a slow process. Eventually we gave up and sat at the edge of the stage and looked at the now grayish mountain being blasted on all sides with fans. Even without paint, I could see the rocky-looking formation emerging.

"It doesn't look like much," Shay said.

"It's a thousand percent better than the chicken wire," I said.

"True," Tessa added. Tessa turned and looked at the empty seats. "We open in a week."

Shay shivered. "You have no idea how grateful I am not to be in this show."

"You would have had fun," I said and bumped her shoulder. "You could have been a pirate with me. Arrgghh!"

Shay crossed her arms. "Nope. Not for me. You have to admit theater is rather esoteric."

Izzy snort-laughed, and I guffawed.

Tessa said, "Shay, you're the best."

"What?" Shay asked. "Esoteric?"

I nodded. "I could google it, but I'm good."

The fans whirred, and for a few moments there was no other sound. I considered the vast auditorium, the shadows growing thicker the deeper the rows went. I didn't know how it would feel being onstage as one of many telling a story. No spotlight on just me. No one but me would know the effort I put into that small pirate part. The mountain. And into Peter. Well, God would know. He saw every moment I had walked through. In a very real way, He'd be in that audience too.

"Everything about this show has been a blast. I want to do it every year," Izzy said.

"Not me," Tessa said. "It's been fun and exciting to be a part of, but juggling swim with this? It's been way too much."

"And Alex," Izzy said.

"And Alex," Tessa admitted.

I stood up and faced the lights, the empty seats before me.

"Junior year, I will get a real part!" I called out.

Izzy jumped up. "Junior year, I will get a million followers!"

Izzy and I looked down at Tessa and Shay.

Tessa stood up and cupped her hands around her mouth, "Junior year, I will . . . get straight A's!"

"Don't you do that every year?" I said.

"Yeah, Tessa. What do you really want?" Shay asked.

Tessa was quiet for a long moment. She turned to the empty audience and said in a soft voice, "I will spend time with my dad and stop feeling angry."

Izzy squeezed Tessa's hand, and then we looked at Shay, who was still sitting on the floor.

Shay cocked her head. "I just want us to stay friends. I'm not trying to be sappy or anything, but, you guys? You've been what I've needed most—and I didn't even know I needed you."

"Me too," Tessa said.

"Same," Izzy said.

"Yep," I added. "This matters. Right here. Us? I've never had friends like you guys. Willing to say things I won't like because you care enough to say what needs to be said. Willing to forgive me when I screw up. Willing to come and help me create a mountain."

"Willing to have my back," Izzy said. "Believe me and stand up for me."

"Willing to see the real me and still love me," Tessa added.

"Willing to step into the unknown with me. Really, I wouldn't have made it through this year without you. Knowing you were right there? It made all the difference," Shay said.

We exchanged Cheshire Cat grins.

"Well, I'm not going anywhere. You guys are totally stuck with me!" I said.

"Same!" everyone said and leaned in for an awkward group hug. When we sat back, Tessa laughed. "We still have to paint that monstrosity!"

"Hey, that monstrosity is my buddy George," I said.

"You named the mountain?" Shay asked.

I shrugged. "Well, we've been spending a lot of time together. I thought he deserved name recognition."

We helped each other up, brushed off the dust, and tackled the mountain together.

Chapter
28

"TECH. WEEK. Now y'all know what I'm talking about, right?" Kenny looked at the cast sprawled around the Darling nursery. "And some of you know what's coming. Tech week. Going through each little piece of the play to make sure we have everything technical down—lights, sound, sets—whatever. It involves lots of waiting. Lots of being ready. Lots of not wandering off. Everyone stays put so you're here when I need you. Got it?"

A loud crash came from the left wing, making everyone jump.

"And please don't get crushed by these flying people. Risa'll kill me if I lose any of her precious students."

Another loud crash.

Kenny cringed. "From the top!"

Kenny sat in the center of the auditorium. I sat in a chair next to the stage, so I could cue a little easier.

The music started, and the curtain opened on the Darling nursery. The boy who played Michael missed a line, so I interrupted, and Kenny had them go back to the beginning of the scene. Peter made his, uh, her entrance. There was this slight pause before Brie said each line as she let her brain connect. I knew what she was doing, so maybe I was simply more aware, but it made the lines feel a little stilted. Unnatural. But saying them was enough of a victory, and I figured we weren't going to get any better.

During my onstage pirate thing, I continued to cue or correct lines.

"Do you have the entire show memorized?" Kenny asked me during a break.

"Yeah. I think so. I didn't really try memorizing it all. It just happened."

—⁓—

We barreled toward opening night with alarming speed. I continued to work hard to help Brie become a wonderful and successful Peter. She continued to improve every rehearsal. Of course, there remained a sliver of longing to play the boy who never grew up. To crow loud and long. But resentment? Jealousy? None at all.

The entire cast watched as the flying crew hoisted Brie into the air for her first flying run. Within minutes she looked completely at ease, looking for all the world like she was truly flying. And I knew.

I knew.

Brie was made for this role. There was no doubt. Brie *was* Peter Pan.

She hollered and shouted as she flipped and soared.

I had pictured myself a thousand times as Peter onstage. In every scene. With every line. But I had not pictured myself in the air. Reality was, I could never do that. Reality was, my Peter would never look like that. Could never have done that.

Then I found out there was a weight limit for the equipment.

In this world where everyone is supposed to accept you just the way you are, I believed being fat shouldn't limit anyone from anything. I could picture a plump Peter like me, joyful and cocky, just as easily as a pixie Peter. But the flying people were limited by the confines of their equipment. I didn't know my actual weight. I didn't really want to know my actual weight. But I was pretty sure it must be more than the equipment allowed. Even if I had gotten the role, my Peter would have been grounded. Those realizations made me feel limited in a way I didn't quite know how to navigate.

Reality was zipping through the air in front of me, the cast shrieking along with Peter. Peter must fly. Brie looked amazing as she flew. Ms. Larkin had been right all along. And so, I had to admit, had God. Yeah, I'd prayed, and I thought I'd listened. But instead I had misinterpreted God's answers. I had assigned ideas and motives to God out of my own stubborn, desperate desires. He had His own plan for my future. I thought I knew what that looked like. No more. Finally, I'd come to a place where I was ready to put my hand in His and go where He takes me. I don't have to chase the spotlight or anything else. I can trust that He is going to take me down the best, most amazing path to . . . to whatever and wherever He wants me to be. Maybe I'll let Him write my story because He knows me best.

Opening night, an electric current of excitement zipped through the cast and crew. Our auditorium was enormous, and ticket sales were strong. People had invested their money to contribute to the miracle of flight on our little stage; everyone was excited to see Peter fly.

I stopped by Brie and Jenna's dressing room—one of the small band practice rooms that had been claimed as dressing rooms. They had their costumes on and were putting the finishing touches on their makeup. Because Brie's straight black bob looked great, we hadn't bothered with the typical red-haired Peter. Red hair wouldn't have looked right on Brie anyway.

I gave Brie a quick hug. "You'll do great. You've been completely fine all week, so you will be completely fine out there. I promise."

She bit her lip and gave me a quick nod in an "I hope you're right" kind of way. "You'll be nearby? Just in case?" she asked.

"Absolutely. You won't need me, but I'll be there."

She sucked in a big breath and let it out slowly, eyes closed.

"You'll be great."

I meant it. She would be great. The effect she would have flying and with the acrobatics would distract people from her weaknesses.

I wish Ms. Larkin had come to the show, so I could tell her that I now understood what she had seen in Brie. But we received word that her mother was still too critical. She wrote that she was sad to miss the show but that she was there with us in spirit.

I then gave Jenna a hug. I didn't know if we'd ever be friends, but it didn't seem as important to be connected anymore. "You're doing a great job as Wendy," I told her.

"Thanks," she said. "For everything."

I closed the door between us and looked at the Wall of Fame. Multicolored stickies curled away from it, each one filled with encouraging, beautiful words. Almost every time I walked by, I saw people standing in front of it, reading, and looking pleased. I had no idea if the Wall really helped change the vibe of what was happening in the cast, but I believed it helped, even if in some small way.

"There you are!" Kenny came up behind me.

I spun around.

Kenny had both hands laced behind his head, giving him elbow wings. He looked frazzled and jumpy. His usual state of affairs was high energy, so it didn't seem out of place. He dropped his hands dramatically and said, "We. Have. A. Problem." He paced in a quick circle, gesturing wildly. "Why, for the love of musical theater everywhere, does Risa not assign understudies? Hmm? Why? Everyone has understudies. You assign understudies for exactly this situation. But no. Not Marisa Larkin. She's all 'God will work it out.' Well, I would like to know what her God's gonna do about this?"

"Kenny. Stop. What's wrong?" I said.

He held up his hand. "I'll show you."

I followed him through the crowded hallways filled with pirates and Lost Boys and Indians back to the set of practice rooms on the other side of the band room. He pointed at the third door. "Mrs. Darling, darlin'."

I walked past Kenny to the last of the three little rooms and poked my head into the open door of Theresa and Eden's dressing room. Eden gave me a nervous look but didn't say anything.

Theresa was fully dressed in her Mrs. Darling costume, makeup finished, hair perfectly up in a poufy bun. But despite the makeup, her face had a grayish tinge, and her eyes looked dead. And she was clutching a bucket to her chest.

"I'm fine," she whispered. "I'll be fine."

Eden shook her head at me slowly, her eyes wide.

"Just nerves. Normal," she choked out.

I looked at Kenny down the hallway, and he shook his head too.

"Hey, Eden. Why don't you get your stuff and go to a different dressing room?" I suggested.

Eden didn't hesitate. She piled stuff in her arms and was gone in a flash.

I didn't want to get too close. Living with my mother had made me germ conscious. "Isolate and disinfect" was her motto. And it worked most of the time. Whatever it was that Theresa had, we didn't need the whole cast getting it. Especially if it was the kind of sickness that required buckets.

"I'll be fi—" she started and then abruptly stopped. I braced myself and turned away in case she started puking, but when I heard nothing, I turned back to see she was slumped on the desk.

"Theresa? Hey? You know you can't go out there, right?"

She turned to look at me without lifting her head from the desk. Her face crumpled, and she started to cry.

"Hey, it's okay. It's okay. I bet it's just a twenty-four-hour thing. If you go home and rest, you might be fine for tomorrow night." I had no idea if that was true, but I thought it was at least reasonable. "Can you text your mom or someone to come get you? You shouldn't be driving."

I helped her get her phone out and texted her mother for her. Then I reached for the Purell dispenser on a nearby table.

"What about the show?" she managed to get out.

"Don't worry about that! You only need to worry about getting home and getting better. We'll take care of everything here."

She nodded weakly and closed her eyes.

I partially closed the door and motioned for Izzy and Tessa, who were sitting in the band room with other ensemble members. They both hurried over.

"Theresa's really sick. Can you guys stay here until her mom gets here? She's on the way. But don't go in unless she needs help. I don't want you guys or anyone else getting whatever she has."

"But . . . she's Mrs. Darling! We need her!" Izzy said.

"I know." I looked for Kenny, but he was gone. "Just make sure she gets out of here, okay? Then close that door and lock it until we can clean it."

"We'll take care of her. Go," Tessa said.

I nodded and hurried through the hallways back to the stage where I found Kenny and Wilson looking up into the rafters.

"Hey."

Kenny turned. "And?"

"Her mom's coming to pick her up," I said. Wilson gave me a questioning look. "Theresa's sick."

He cringed. "And no understudies."

"I know!" Kenny said. "Risa and I are gonna have it out on this one."

I took a deep breath. "I can do it," I said.

Kenny gave me a double take and then stared at me for a long moment saying nothing. "You know the lines, don't you?"

Wilson laughed, "She knows the whole thing."

"Yeah. Pretty sure I can do the lines," I said.

Kenny raised an eyebrow at me. "What about the song?"

I nodded, saying nothing. I was a lot less confident about the song.

"It's not like we have a lot of choices. Let's see what you can do, pirate."

Chapter
29

WE FOUND MRS. RINALDI in the band room sitting at the old grand piano that looked so scuffed up and well-worn that we thought maybe the school had been built around it. It still sounded beautiful though.

She was playing scales for the cluster of leads who were warming up their vocals.

I followed Kenny. When he leaned on the piano, she stopped playing. She seemed irritated by Kenny in general, so I wasn't surprised when she snapped, "What? I'm doing warm-ups."

He gestured to me. "We need her to be Mrs. Darling because our Mrs. Darling is puking her guts out."

Mrs. Rinaldi opened her mouth at me and looked like she was trying to decide if that was a good idea or a bad one. "Can you sing?" she asked.

Something about the way she asked drained the tiny bit of confidence I'd had. I half nodded, half shrugged.

"Make it work. Even if she has to do it like a monologue," Kenny said. He turned to me. "I'm gonna have Mrs. Copeland find you something to wear."

Kenny left, and Mrs. Rinaldi pinched her lips as she looked at me. After a moment she said, "Let's warm you up."

She played some scales, and I tried to follow along. She acted like I should know how to do certain things with my breath and diaphragm and was exasperated when she had to explain them to me. I tried not to let her negativity bother me, but by the time we got to practice the actual song, I felt rattled.

Then I noticed Izzy, Tessa, and Shay standing in the door-way watching. When I looked over, they waved and gave me a thumbs-up. They looked so happy for me. Tessa mouthed, "You've got this."

I nodded. *I've got this. I can do this.* It didn't matter if Mrs. Rinaldi believed in me or not. I could do this.

Mrs. Rinaldi played the opening notes to "Tender Shepherd," and my first few lines were really shaky. I wasn't breathing. That was the big thing I learned in the couple of voice lessons I had taken. You had to have enough breath in your lungs for the notes to come out clear and strong. Next time I got to a breathing part, I took in extra air. What a difference! It was far less wobbly and even sounded . . . okay. Mrs. Rinaldi finished the song but didn't look convinced.

"Let's do it again," I said. The second time through, I made sure I breathed at the correct spots, and it was a little more okay than before.

I glanced over at the girls, and they were still smiling and nodding.

"One more time?" I asked.

The third time through, Mrs. Rinaldi worked with me and gave me pointers at a couple of spots. When we finished, she shrugged. "You'll do."

Yes, I would.

I hurried over to the girls. They hugged me and peppered me with encouragement. "You're going on?" "This is so exciting!" "That would be terrifying!" The last comment was from Shay, of course, but she followed it up with, "I'm happy for you, though!"

Mrs. Copeland arrived with a handful of skirts and tops. After gathering makeup and hair supplies, the four of us went to one of the dressing rooms that had emptied to turn me into Mrs. Darling.

Tessa and Shay went through the clothes trying to match something while Izzy started pulling at my hair.

"You know, your long hair would have been perfect to have an updo like Theresa had," Izzy said.

"True. But I think I like being a red-haired Edna Mode," I said.

"Glad to hear it," Izzy laughed. "You would rock as Edna Mode."

Izzy somehow managed to pin my hair in a way that made it look sort of like an updo. Tessa and Shay paired a long blue skirt with a printed button-down top that looked matronly on me. Just the look needed for the Mom role.

When we finished, I held out my arms and did a slow spin while they assessed the finished product.

"Yep!" Izzy said.

"Perfect!" Tessa said.

Shay cocked her head. "I'm very impressed with you right now."

Another group hug. Shay nudged me. "Come on, we have to get your mic and do your sound check."

Izzy and Tessa waved goodbye, and Shay led me to the mic table where Anthony was waiting for me.

"Hurry up! They want to open the house," he said.

"She's doing the best she can!" Shay snapped at him.

Shay fed the wire down my shirt and helped me get the mic taped to my face and clipped the mic pack to the inside back of my skirt. Then she led me to the deserted stage, the spotlights on the nursery behind me. There was no mic stand now, just an open stage and a vast, empty audience. I could practically feel the anticipation crackle through the air.

I stepped into the light and took a long slow breath.

"You ready?" Wilson's voice echoed through the sound system from the booth where I knew he was sitting.

"I hope so," I said.

"You'll be amazing," he said.

"Thanks."

"Say a couple of lines," he instructed.

We did that with two or three lines as he adjusted the sound.

"Now give me some of the song," he said.

I hesitated. I could do this. I was going to be singing in front of an enormous audience in less than an hour. I couldn't be scared to do it in front of Wilson. I pushed aside the flutters and made sure I took in enough breath.

I sang the first verse a cappella.

"Fabulous. Break a leg, Mrs. Darling." And then he paused. "We'll celebrate with a smoothie tomorrow—if you're free."

"Yeah," I said with a quiet confidence. "I'd like that."

As we stood ready in our places, we could hear the kids and the excited audience through the thick, red velvet curtain that separated *Peter Pan* from the auditorium. I knew my parents were out there, along with Josh and Jessica. Even Maggie had driven in to watch. In those moments, in the breath before the orchestra began the overture, I had become a part of the electricity, the excitement. Our cast had a beautiful story to share. The story of a boy who believes. Of orphans and mothers. Of magic and flying. I wasn't dressed as Peter Pan like I had imagined so many times. I was dressed as an adult woman. A mom. But I was a part of the story. An important part.

I knew that it was possible the real Mrs. Darling would feel better in the morning. I likely only had one night. One night to embrace it all.

The curtains slid open, and the light illuminated my upturned face.

And embrace it I did.